EARTH'S GUARDIANS

THE AMBASSADOR CHRONICLES

VOLUME I

ISBN: 978-8-218-19550-2 (Paperback)

Any references to historical events, real people, or real places are used fictitiously. Names, characters, and places are products of the author's imagination.

Front cover image by Mary Wright, www.fiverr.com/mary_k_wright

Book design by HMDpublishing

First printing edition 2023.

t.davis@841fadmedia.org

Acknowledgements

First and foremost, I would like to give honor to God who is the head of my life for his grace, strength, sustenance and above all, His faithfulness and love.

To my family thank you for the inspiration, the character examples ☺ and the push! I love you all. To my sons Tavaris and Alonzo for the motivation throughout this project, and always asking me is the book done yet to keep me on task. I'm proud to be your dad! To my little crew, my heartbeats, Amerah, Adam, Andrew, Alex, Leo and Aiden. Pop Pop loves all of you to the moon and back.

To Frank and Edna Davis, you both planted this writing seed in me when I was a teenager. I was so blessed to have you as parents, I wish you were here to share in this. Love you!!

To my crew, Derick (717 ImaginaryHouse Comix Ent) and Charrs (Diuniverse Comics) thanks for reigniting the fire for this project, the honest feedback, the great advice, and the great collaboration, I can't wait for the time our worlds collide on paper!

Most of all I would like to thank my wife Angelina, for being an intricate part in making this dream happen. Thank you for the encouragement, the motivation, the honest feedback, the push when the project was stalling and those key words that kept me going. Love you Mrs. Davis and it's 841 until the wheels fall off!!!

About the Author

A native Memphian, author Terrell Davis attended Hamilton High School. After graduation, he attended Alabama State University where he obtained a bachelor's degree in accounting. He continued his education at Union University and received a master's degree in business administration.

Professionally, Terrell has been an investment analyst for Memphis Light, Gas and Water. He has served on various boards; he is an officer with East Trigg Baptist church and President of 841 FAD Media. A loving husband, proud father of two and grandfather of six. Thrilled to be blessed with this opportunity to start this journey.

CONTENTS

CHAPTER 01
THE ORIGIN

Year – 2041, Date August 4th 10:15 AM Washington D.C.

Houston's frustration was painfully evident as he sat in front of the communications terminal, awaiting a report from Boom and Mac who were doing reconnaissance outside of the White House because of high alien activity. The black screen suddenly came to life with a shaky image that left no doubt that the men were moving in on their location. Just then static erupted announcing that the comm links were coming online. Houston then heard Boom's deep voice; he was trying his best to whisper.

"Houston do you read me?"

"I hear you loud and clear Boom what is your status?"

Marcel Brown better known as Boom was a stocky 6-foot 3 bald man with a full beard. His presence was the definition of intimidation, it didn't help that he kept a scowl on his face at all times with his signature unlit cigar hanging from the corner of his mouth. His teammate in all the ops he has been on was Marcus McDonald better known as Mac. Mac was a tall man he stood 6 foot 3 and is built like an NFL quarterback. His light brown eyes, radical blond hair and strong jaw line was always an eye catcher of the opposite sex. Mac may be a ladies' man, but he had one thing in common with Boom. If you contested them in any way, you would not survive. They were ex special forces. Mac was an expert sniper and a communications and weapons specialist. Boom was an expert sniper and an explosive expert. They had several tours of duty under their belts and were well known for making it out of unbelievably sticky situations without a scratch. Most people believed that the pair would be lifelong special forces members, but corruption in the military forced them out and led them to join the Houston's Scorpion group.

Suddenly the images on the screen stopped shaking, Houston could now clearly see Booms bearded face. His eyes were gapped wide open with intensity, he and Mac were using some type of brush as cover. Houston could make out alien ships moving over their heads.

"Boom and Mac It looks really crowded there." Said Houston.

Boom gave a sarcastic look into the camera, then blurted into his comm link. "You think!" "It is just too many of these damn alien sidewinders moving around. My trigger finger is itching like crazy. Now is as good a time than any for the ambassadors to drop in!"

"The triplets, how bad is it?" Houston shouted while rising from his chair.

Boom now wiping sweat off his brow. Whispered through clinched teeth.

"Yes, the ambassadors!! "The buildings empty except for the President and a few men; and now we have incoming aliens, we need them now!"

Houston was now leaning over his monitor. "Boom show me what you are seeing!"

Boom angled his 16K camera toward the White House. What Houston saw was like something out of the movies. The wind around the White House lawn began to pick up as paper and shrubbery were being blown around. A large dark grey alien ship in the shape of a falcon in midflight touched down on the front lawn. The hull of the ship glimmered in the light as if the hull were created with some sort of metallic glass. Houston could feel his heart rate increase with every second of the ship touching down. He nervously blurted out. "Okay that's a very disturbing image, any idea why they landed?"

All Houston could hear was silence, deafening silence that was lasting far too long. "Mac! Boom! Come in, are you still there?!" Houston said with a slight panic in his voice.

Mac responded. "Not sure why they landed, but I bet it has something to do with President Taylor being inside the building."

Just then part of the alien craft under carriage opened and a lift lowered the queen, another female alien, five of her guardians and several foot soldiers to the ground. They headed straight for the doors of the white House. Houston was now pacing back and forth in front of his screen.

"Boom and Mac we need to hear and see everything that happens inside that building right damn now!"

Mac looked in his bag, "that shouldn't be a problem, Squirt equipped us with what we need to tap into the buildings security feed."

Boom covers his mic, his face so close to Macs, that Mac could feel every breath.

"I don't like this Mac we should be spraying aliens right now, not patching into no damn security system."

"Boom calm the hell down it is just two of us were severely outnumbered!"

Boom turns to see the last alien passing through the White House front door. He cocks his rifle. Then turns back to Mac. "When has us being outnumbered ever mattered!"

He began to rise out of the brush when Mac grabbed him by his shoulder. Mac now staring directly into boom eyes whispers.

"For the Presidents sake let's find out what's going on inside the building first. When the President is secure, then we can spill all the alien blood your heart desires."

Their comm links chirped to life with Houston's voice.

"Come on men we are losing precious time! I need eyes and ears on the President now!"

Mac and boom could hear the urgency in his voice. Mac stumbles to his feet realizing they were still numb from kneeling in the shrubbery for so long.

"Houston give me a couple of minutes to get in position." Mac checks his surroundings, seeing everything is clear he bolts from their hiding spot shouting. "Boom get your ass moving!"

Boom could hear and see the alien ships still circling overhead. It was difficult to move quickly with all their equipment and stay out of sight. He could feel his legs burning with each stride. He lets out some of his frustration over the comm link.

"Damn a video Houston we need the ambassadors here! It's damn clear we are headed for a fire fight; we need some back up with all these aliens."

The anticipation of seeing what was happening in the White House was becoming unbearable for Houston.

He quickly responded to Boom. "I hear you loud and clear, the S22 ship is about 15 minutes out!" "I will see if I can speed them up, just let me know when you have the video."

Houston was the son of military scientist. His mother and father did extensive work in the bioscience field and made billions of dollars off the sale of their discoveries to pharmaceutical firms. Houston was born after the family fortune was made giving him a unique upbringing; being raised by rich brilliant military parents. Houston often refers to himself as a perfectionist with control issues and often blames this on his upbringing. He followed in his parent's footsteps becoming a military scientist.

His brilliance proceeded him in his career as he began to climb the military ladder. Once he became an officer in the Army, he saw evidence of corruption. Corruption that stemmed from a terrorist group called Arcane, who's roots were spreading throughout all branches of the military and Government. Since Houston did not know who he could trust, he decided to leave the military and fight the corruption from the outside. He decided to use his billion-dollar trust fund to create a group of like-minded individuals equipped with a well-hidden very extensive base of operations in the Arizona desert. A base that was packed to the gills with state-of-the-art weapons and vehicles. He named the group The Scorpions. Their objective was to draw out and eliminate Arcane members. The group had become so proficient at this, that parts of the government began to rely on their services. This was one of those moments.

Right now, his control issues were taking over, he had to end the back-and-forth conversation with Mac and Boom because the results he wanted were not happening soon enough. Meanwhile Boom and Mac snaked their way through the White House grounds, staying out of sight of the aliens moving around. They managed to make it to the main security station without being seen. Boom set up in one of the windows facing the doors of the building. As the lookout he scanned their surroundings through the scope of his gun ready to spill alien blood. Mac was busy quickly connecting Squirt's equipment with the building's security network. Boom pauses to see what Mac was doing.

"So, Squirt taught you how to hack the security system huh?"

Wiping the sweat from his face, Mac quickly responded, holding up one of Squirts tablets. "Nope he gave me his program, I just plug this into the network; hit go and it is just like Squirt is here hacking their system."

The tablet immediately lit up when it connected to the network. A huge green press here to go button appeared on the tablet screen. Mac touched the screen and Squirt's program went to work.

The S22 ship was Houston's pride and joy. A remarkable ship that defies current technology. It is the only ship known with the ability to cloak itself making it virtually undetectable during flight. It is also, one of the fastest aircraft inside and outside of Earth's atmosphere. The frame of the ship was a marriage between the retired space shuttle and a F-22 Raptor aircraft. It was 200 feet tall and 96 feet in diameter with 3 levels inside and equipped with an ungodly arsenal of weapons. The captain of this vessel and the leader of Houston's crew is Chris Barnes but referred to as CB by everyone. He was currently piloting the S22, easily pulling 15 Gees headed towards the White House.

During down times for the ship, the crew is constantly upgrading the equipment and software to ensure that the ship was operating with cutting edge technology. There are several hologram projectors located on all levels of the ship. They all lit up simultaneously with images of an obviously concerned Houston.

The urgency in his voice really stood out.

"CB what is your current location?"

"Houston we are about 4 minutes out." "How are things going in DC?"

"Things are getting very dicey there." Everyone could hear the concern in Houston's voice when he said that.

CB throttled the engines on the ship increasing their flight speed, then blurted into his comm link.

"We are a few clicks away, what the hell is happening?"

"Well CB we currently have an alien ship parked on the white House lawn! This damn alien Queen and her goons are inside with the President!" "So, CB this has now become a rescue mission!"

"Mac and Boom are currently patching into the security system as we speak, I need you and your crew sitting on go when you arrive!"

"Yes sir!" CB shouted. He then turns to his copilot Squirt.

"Okay Squirt cloak the ship now and slow us to mark 2."

The crew could hear Houston holding a conversation with what sounded like Mac, but they could not make out what was being said. Suddenly Houston's voice came through loud and clear.

"CB I am patching you all into Mac's feed at the White House."

The screens on the ship went black for a few seconds then suddenly the appearance of aliens moving through the empty White House halls was all anyone could see. The aliens were moving through the building like they knew every inch of it. Houston broke the silence that was hanging in the air. "Mac we need to see what's happening in the oval office."

Mac quickly responded, "give me a few seconds, I can get video and audio in there!"

Mac made a few taps on the tablet and images from the oval office appeared. President Taylor was standing behind his desk with a handful of Navy Seals armed and ready for battle.

CB franticly responds to what he is witnessing. "Why the hell is President Taylor meeting with these beings? Did he sleep through the last few months where they have crippled our military?"

Boom shouts at CB. "You just hurry up and get here and we can ask him."

Houston chimes in to shut down the argument brewing. "Hey, we need radio silence to hear what is happening."

Inside the oval office the men could hear the footsteps of the aliens getting closer.

There was eerie laughter coming from the hallways, as the footsteps grew louder. The leader of the Navy Seals squad looks at President Taylor.

"Sir I don't like this. Let us move you to a secure location."

President Taylor obviously disturbed with what he was hearing coming down the hallway. Looked at the soldier with concern. He took a deep breath and wiped his face. "I don't like this either, but they asked for this meeting with me. This may be our only chance to stop this invasion. We owe this to all Americans who died or are suffering from this invasion! You and your men just be ready for Anything!" The leader snaped back "Sir yes sir!" He turned to his men, "give me two men at the door now." Two of the Seals immediately took positions on either side of the office door which was partially open.

"Remember men we don't react; we attack be ready for anything." Before anyone could respond to that, both doors swung open violently. The two men by the doors aimed their M16 at what was coming in the door. Everyone aboard the S22 ship gasped simultaneously at what they saw. Radio silence ended with Houston shouting,

"Oh my God!"

Boom quickly responded, "So much for freaking peace!"

Houston responded screaming "Engage, engage get to the President now!"

Boom looks at Mac and shouts "Finally!"

They both bolt out of the security booth in opposite directions. They see the alien ships maneuvering like they are targeting something. Mac could hear the engines of the S22 screaming overhead. He could not see the ship because it was cloaked but he did see three bodies appear out of thin air.

Finally, the Ambassadors were joining the fight! Houston who was across the country in Arizona, plopped down in his chair knowing there was nothing he could do to help. All he could do was wait to hear from someone. He took a deep breath trying to calm his nerves. His mind began to race thinking of the possible outcomes, he couldn't help but to reflect on how they all got to this moment.

CHAPTER 02
THE COVER UP

Year - 2023

Politicians are still debating if the last three years of natural disasters are due to global warming or not. One thing the world quickly found out was how outdated its infrastructure and power grids were. Three solid years of hurricanes, typhoons, earthquakes, and flooding has pushed most of the world to extreme measures just to have some sense of what we are used to in everyday life. The destruction caused a shortage in natural fuel sources and contaminated 30 percent of our drinking water. The race has begun to find clean fuel that runs on a platform that will coexist with the new standards needed for infrastructure. The fact that several nuclear facilities were pushed to the brink of complete failure from these events; made it clearly obvious the world needs a new source of energy. The race increased tenfold based on an actual accident by the US space program. Star port Vegas was created to further the United States exploration in space study. The largest space station known to man; it was the size of a major US city. Built in the shape of a round diamond, the station was completely occupied by our military and NASA officers. The station is equipped with an arsenal of weapons to protect it. Photon cannons and cameras lined the outside of the station in all directions. Equipped with two Heli pads four times the size of the L.A.X. airport; star port Vegas was capable of launching and landing cargo ships, talons, fighter ships, drones and satellites. Attached to the space station by a long bridge that stretched 100 yards was the construction site for the Horizon.

NASA decided to launch one of their drone ships called Cardinal-1 to study Saturn's moon Titan, because Titan has a lot of Earths characteristics. This was in response to the problems the International Space Program was having with inhabiting Mars. The Mars program was becoming very expensive with little success. They were hoping that Titan would be a more fitting site to begin expanding mankind's presence in the Milky Way. Midway through its trip NASA discovered that Cardinal-1 flight course was headed directly into the path of a meteor shower. The meteor shower was vast in size capable of destroying anything in its path. Now Cardinal-1 was twice the size of its predecessor the stealth bomber. It was equipped with the capabilities of nimble flight maneuvers like ships much smaller than it; but in this situation there was no possible way for the ship to avoid this meteor storm. It will definitely rip the ship into pieces. There was only one option for the ship to avoid being ripped to shreds and that would be to use its hyper drive system. The hyper drive system was in its infancy stages; it had been tested on smaller ships in controlled environments with decent results; but not like this. Not with a ship this size at this rate of speed. Facing the option of losing the ship and all its cargo to destruction the scientist decided to use the hyper drive to jump to the outer edge of Titans atmosphere. They had the target location pinpointed and when the coordinates are entered into Cardinal-1 system the ship should make its jump. It would fall off their radar for a few hours and appear again rotating around Titan. That is what should have happened; to this day they do not know what caused the incident. Was it the size of the ship, or its speed? Did they miscalculate the distance from the meteor shower? Whatever it was it caused Cardinal-1 to lose contact for three full days. When the ship reappeared on the radar it had overshot Titan and was now on the outer edge of our solar system. An attempt to save the ship from being destroyed by meteors had resulted in it being lost in space. That was the thinking until Cardinal-1 regained its communication abilities with the NASA control center. The ship began delivering photos of an uncharted planet. The planet was smaller than earth but had a lot of similarities. The drone was close enough to the surface too detect unique terrain and large bodies of what looked like water. Scientist believed that this new uncharted planet was outside of our galaxy. A team of brother and sister astronomers were the only two people present when Cardinal-1 began transmitting information. The Washington siblings immediately began charting this new discovery and, because of that, they were given the honor of naming the planet. After a heated debate they agreed to name it Gema Oculta which means hidden gem. The drone Cardinal-1 was built to withstand the worst of the worst conditions known to man. It was designed specifically to explore newly discovered environments, which is the main reason the ship was dumping hundreds of pictures on to the control centers network drive. The group agreed since there was a high probability that they could not get Cardinal-1 back to Earth, it could be beneficial to explore this new planet. They decided to instruct the ship to land close to what was believed to be a body of water and explore from the shore inland. They instructed Cardinal-1 to follow a descent plan, now it takes around one full day for the control room to receive any pictures or data from Cardinal-1. The next morning the control center main monitors came to life with picture after picture from Cardinal-1. The drone had safely touched down on the surface of Gema and began taking pictures of its surroundings. The high-powered camera that it was equipped with produced some vibrant breath-taking images. The surface around the drone looked like a billion saucers sized grey smooth rocks, with violet spheres sprinkled throughout in every direction. The terrain was flat from the ship's location to the water line. The water had a slight tint to it that was the same color grey as the rocks on the shore. Leading away from the shore the rocks led up to a huge plush dark green hillside that led to mountains that were black as coal. The Cardinal-1 released its rover to test the atmosphere and gather soil and water samples. The rover was equipped with oversized tank wheels that function well on many different surfaces; it slowly made its way over the unsteady terrain to the edge of the body of water. The water was very still, it reflected everything around it like a huge mirror. The rover was unable to see below the surface of the water to take any pictures. So, the rover launched two DPSP sensors to get readings one on the shore and one in the water. The sensor on land immediately began transmitting data. It detected a low presence of oxygen in the atmosphere, as well as carbon dioxide and hydrogen. Those were the only elements the system was able to recognize. The sensors were twelve-inch tubes with transmitting antennas; they are covered in small black data point smart panels that resembled miniature solar panels. The land sensors were also equipped with balloons to keep them airborne for a period of time. The liquid sensors have hydrometers connected to them to measure the density of the liquid by keeping a portion of the tube submerged right below the surface. The DPSP that landed in the body of liquid could not detect any of the elements contained in it. The scientists were busy trying to figure out what the unknown elements detected by the DPSP sensors could possibly be; until the rover had an encounter with one of the violet spears. That encounter took precedent over all their other work. The rover collected one of the spears and placed it in its testing chamber. The chamber is how the rover was able to closely examine any materials it collects. The video that played for everyone at the command center was very dimly lit. All the equipment on Gema was operating on low settings to conserve energy because the solar panels were not collecting much energy in this foreign atmosphere. Everything was going according to plan until the rover added water to the chamber to clean the spear. There was an immediate reaction; it appeared as if the spear was boiling in the water. The lights inside the chamber began to get brighter and brighter until they burst. The reaction lasted for a couple of minutes ending just as fast as it started. When the engineers checked the status on the equipment all the rover energy readings were maxed out. The questions to answer now was, were these spears capable of producing clean energy? Based on the current readings from the drone's equipment that small reaction generated enough energy to power a small city. The US Government wanted to keep this information quiet, but everyone working on interpreting the data from this project had to enlist help from all around the world. There was simply too much information for one group to go through; plus, it would be very difficult to keep a possible abundant source of clean energy quiet. The sharing of information is what began the race to terraform the planet, Gema.

The Regan military base was designed to feature life on Gema. Every aspect of space travel and the planet had been considered in its design. This is where Houston and Tory Prototype program will begin. The Prototype program is designed to develop soldiers to defeat any opposition to US claimed soil on this newfound planet. General McClain entered the office where Houston and Tory were unpacking. "Gentlemen" McClain shouted as he entered the room, startling the men. "I want to make sure we have a clear understanding on what the purpose is for this program!" Tory stepped forward "General I believe our objectives have been made clear."

"Well Tory in my book when you say I believe you do not understand the gravity of your objectives." "Have a seat." The General pulled up a seat across the table from the two men. "I want the two of you to understand that this is a race to be the first to terraform this newly discovered planet. This race will not be won by which country has the best scientist, or best equipment. This race will be won by the country that is capable of defending its borders with the biggest and best soldiers known to man. In two years, the Horizon will have its first test launch. That means we have roughly 2 to 3 years before the United States starts its terraforming. You gentlemen have less time than that to create a program that will develop the men and women we need to ensure success of this project." Tory stood up to address the General. "Sir we have had great success with our trial runs of the Prototype project!" Tory dropped a large notebook on the table. "Here are some of the results." "We are expecting better results as we take the trials full scale with these soldiers."

'Yes, Tory I have seen the trial results." The General responded while thumbing through the notebook. He turned his attention to Houston. "So, Houston you have been very quiet, do you share the same sentiments as your colleague Tory?" Houston took a long look at Tory before responding." I have to be more realistic than Tory, any time you go to human trials there is always the possibility for setbacks. Color me optimistic that we will be able to accomplish this in your time frame." Tory tried to interrupt Houston before he said anything else. "Sir we are ready to overcome any problems that may arise during these trials!" The General waved his hand to silence Tory. "One of you is positively sure of success and the other is optimistic. Understand that I don't give a damn about any of that; we are not paying you for your feelings!" The General then popped up out of his seat; standing there he puts an unlit cigar in his mouth while staring down at the men. "Gentlemen, we are paying you for results and that is what I am expecting, Results!!" He turned to walk out of the room but suddenly stopped at the door. "By the way, when will some of the results with these live trials be available?" Tory quickly responded, "we have twelve candidates for the first trial, which should last between six to nine weeks. We should have some serious results to present after that time frame." The General turns to face both men. "What I am hearing gentlemen is that in two months you will have all of the data necessary to provide me with a program that will churn out unstoppable warriors in a year." Houston stood up "sir that is not what he said!" The General took a long stern look at the two men.

"That's funny because I am sure that's what I heard; good day gentlemen." Tory waited for the door to close and seal before responding. "Houston why the hell would you say that there are chances for setbacks to the General?"

"Because I truly believe there are Tory. You cannot seriously think that this will go off without any problems; and to further complicate things we are now on this acid timeline made up by the General." "Mistakes are bound to happen. I understand your concerns but Houston, I really need you to have more confidence in our team. Whatever happens here we are prepared and highly capable of handling. You need to get on the same page as your team."

"The same page? I still don't believe any of this is legal, and if it goes south who do you think the blame will fall on. Not the General or the US Government, because our names are the ones all over this project."

"Houston, just trust me your concerns are mine as well, but we are being paid a lot of money to get this done. Our reputation as scientist and doctors are on the line."

"That is just it Tory we started this to help mankind not for money or recognition, I believe we have lost our way."

"What the hell, lost our way? So, what in the world do you suggest we do?"

"I know this will sound crazy, but we put the brakes on this project long enough for us to step back and clearly access what we are doing here." Tory who was pacing back and forth for the whole conversation comes to a stop directly in front of Houston. "Houston you have got to be freaking playing with me. You wait until zero hour to start talking about stepping back and accessing the situation, HAVE YOU LOST YOUR DAMN MIND!"

"Tory you need to calm down."

"Don't freaking tell me to calm down. What the hell do you think we have been doing the past five years with this project? Everything we have done is for this moment and now of all times Houston you want to play scared."

"Now Tory I didn't say I was scared."

"Well, what you just said damn sure sounds like your scared!"

Houston lets out a deep sigh and takes a seat in one of the chairs in the middle of the room. Staring at the floor he responds. "It is not fear it is concern, concern that all of this is moving way to fast. Knowing the history of our government when they want things in a hurry it is never for what they share with you; it is always for something far more sinister." Houston hears a loud UGGGHHH from Tory. He then rolls a chair in front of Houston and takes a seat. "Listen to me Houston, life moves at a swift pace and with the current events happening in this world that pace has reached supersonic speed. The truth of the matter is humans will colonize Gema in the next few years with or without this program. Here we sit with an opportunity to ensure life for this country carries on for our future loved ones. So, Houston, who else do you trust with a project like this? WHO? I will answer that question for you. NO ONE!" "That's right Houston only our team. I can assure you we are prepared for whatever the General has up his sleeve." Houston sat back in his chair and looked up to the ceiling before answering. "Now that is true Tory, we are prepared for anything." "But I Have Just one question for you," he was now staring directly at Tory. "What are you prepared to do if this fails?" Tory was trying to keep his cool during this discussion, but that one word had him on the brink of losing it. He felt the urge to grab Houston and shake some sense into him. Tory rolled back in his chair to put some distance between them. With a shocked face he yells "FAILS!" "That will not happen. There is not a possibility of that, and we are not having this conversation!"

Tory walks across the room to the intercom system still repeating his last words. "Nope we are not having this conversation!"

"Tory that is another one of my concerns, you are unwilling to accept reality about this project."

"Houston we are not having this freaking conversation, you are starting to piss me off." Tory punched in a code on the intercom and a young attractive female appeared on screen. "Mr. Drew, how may I be of assistance."

"Have all of the participants in Prototype 01 been checked in?"

"Yes sir, they have been getting settled into their barracks, but they are ready to be addressed by you and Mr. Creed. Should I summon them?"

"Yes, have the group ready to meet with us in conference room B in 15 minutes."

"Yes sir!" The screen goes black, and Tory turns to Houston. "This is starting now, with or without you, I need to know if you are on board."

"Tory, we need to have that conversation."

"No Houston, what we need to do is get started on this project, we have a lot of work ahead and the General shaved off some of our time. So again, I ask, Houston are you on board?" Houston stood there in silence for what seemed like an eternity before he responded. He could feel his conscious telling him this will not end well with the General, but he knew that they were on the brink of a serious scientific breakthrough. Conflicted he weakly responded to Tory. "Yes, I am on board."

"Good, then let's go to work!" The two men exit the room and make their way to the elevators. Tory and Houston exit an elevator on sub level B. They walked through the typical dark grey concrete walls that lined almost every military installation. The facility was built to be functional not astatically pleasing.

The two men arrived at a large black metal door that stood about 8 feet high. They paused for a few seconds before Tory broke the silence. "Well, my friend this is the beginning of a new world, and we are the authors." Houston let out a sigh before responding. "Yeah, I hope this new world is far more sensible than our current one." The two men entered the room through the large door to see the volunteers sprawled all over the room. As usual Houston found a seat near the door, while Tory stood at the front of the room to address the volunteers. "Excuse me may I have your attention. Let me be the first one to officially welcome all of you to Regan Air Force base." "I am Tory Drew and my colleague to my right is Houston Creed; we are part of the group running this program. I want to personally thank you for volunteering for the Prototype project, this project would not exist without everyone in this room."

At that moment, a hand in the back of the room shot up. "Hey Doc so you two are like some super geniuses right?"

Tory smiled at that question "well my background is human genetics and bioengineering; Houston's is human genetics and computer engineering. Geniuses we are not but we are very good at what we do!" A female voice from the center of the group, joined the conversation. "Why is this group called dagger?" Tory smiled at the young lady before answering. "Now that is dagger with one g, which is short for the Department of Advanced Genetics Exploration Research. The wonderful name giving to us by our lovely government, but no one wants to say that all day, so we shortened it." Tory then turned and nodded to Houston. Houston pulled a remote from his lab coat pocket and used it to turn on a device above Tory's head. Houston casually began to speak as he joined Tory at the front of the room. "Are there any more questions before we get into why you all are here?" The room falls silent. "Great, now Tory please dim the lights a little for me." The three-dimensional hologram projector lit up with images that filled the front of the room. Houston gave a brief history lesson on how the project reached this point. "Ladies and gentlemen one of NASA's satellites happened to pass closely by a huge asteroid that we believe originated in the Novalucent galaxy which is estimated to be over 15 million light years away from our solar system. In passing by the asteroid our satellite captured images of some odd growths on it. An unmanned probe was sent to investigate, and to our surprise there were frozen plants all over the asteroid. The probe gathered as many of the plants that it could safely without damaging them. The plants were taken to star port Vegas to be studied. Once there, the plants were thawed out and exposed to our atmosphere. Surprisingly, they flourished, especially when they were exposed to sunlight. The silky black plant you see before you is the one of importance. Our scientist preformed further test on this plant and their discovery is why we are all here." "An extract from the black plant, when combined with human DNA, creates heightened reflexes, strength, speed, cognitive reasoning, and awareness. Tory and I engineered a nanite program to be utilized with this plant extract that will enable the volunteer to manage their new abilities almost effortlessly." All the hands went up in the room eagerly wanting to ask a question. Houston had to calm the room down; by waving his hands in the motion to signal a vehicle to slow down. His voice now elevated cut through the mumbling that began when the volunteers raised their hands. "Now wait, wait before we start taking your questions there are some things I need to address. We have you here to perfect our nanite program. Earlier I said almost effortlessly, we are not there yet; but with your assistance we can accomplish just that. Now I can answer your questions?" A white male sitting on the front row blurted out "one simple question doc, are you going to turn us into superheroes?" The room erupts in laughter. Tory walks in front of Houston and the images clapping his hands. "Ladies and gentlemen please hear me when I say this. I don't know if we can create heroes because frankly, they are not real, but we will turn all of you into the greatest soldiers known to man. Can you work with that?" The white male quickly responded, "just one problem doc we are already the greatest soldiers known to man!" The room erupted with cheers. Tory smiling makes a hand gesture to quiet the room down.

"Ok, well then let's just say we will turn you into the group that the greatest soldiers known to man fear." The male quickly responds. "Yeah doc, that sounds about right, everything under God will fear us!" he shouted, while giving high five to the soldiers around him. Houston chimed in, "okay if you want to be the most feared then let's get started." The back doors to the room opened, and eight male and female nurses entered the room, along with Dr. Springer and other staff members. Tory brought everyone's attention back to the front of the room when he began speaking. "Before we leave this room let me introduce you to these individuals that you will get to know very well during your time here." "First this is Tony Jet." A 6-foot 2 man stepped forward and turned to face the group. He looked as if he was chiseled out of granite. His face was stern with a strong jaw line. His expression was as if he was snarling at the group.

"Mr. Jet will oversee training you on hand to hand and weapons combat. He is an expert in martial arts and trust me none of you in this room can take him and you probably never will." Next is Mrs. Alicia Russian and Mr. Steve Barron." A 5-foot blond, white woman who looked more like a model than a trainer entered the room along with a 6-foot well-built white male. "These two will be in charge of PT and weight training, and I promise before this is over you will all hate their guts." The two both smiled and nodded in agreement. "Finally, we have Dr. Raphael Springer." A beautiful caramel complexion woman walked to the front of the room. "Now soldiers she is here to make sure you all are physically and mentally doing ok with the program. Her advisement of your mental and physical health is final; there is no one in this facility that has the authority to overrule her decisions. Simply put, you do exactly what she says, or you will no longer be a part of the program and forfeit your bonuses. Is that understood." The room erupted with a YES SIR!!!!!! "Now these nurses are here to prep you for your cryochambers. I will let Dr. Springer explain." "Thank you, Tory," Raphael said while stepping forward to the front of the group. "Simply put the chambers are designed to slow your heart rate and maintain your body in a state of stasis while we administer the prototype serum. These chambers will also be your sleep pods; they will constantly monitor your vitals as well as provide you with pure oxygen to help in your bodies' development and recovery. You will be inside these chambers for 10 to 12 hours a day." A female voice from the middle of the group responds. "What the hell are we supposed to do in a coffin for 12 hours?" Raphael smiled while glancing back at the group. "You just met your trainers, trust me when they get started with you, all you will want to do is sleep for more than 12 hours in these chambers." Raphael clapped her hands to get everyone's attention. "Okay let's get started everyone strip down to your under wear; don't be shy we will all get to know one another very well in this project. I need the men to my left and the women to my right and my people get them checked out and assigned to a chamber as soon as possible please, thank you." The room erupted with motion and conversations. Raphael turned to Houston and Tory. "Well gentlemen there is no turning back now." Tory twisted up his face to that statement. "Why would we turn back we have worked far too hard and long for these moments. The question is how soon do we start to see results?"

Raphael moved in closer to Tory and Houston so no one could overhear their conversation. "Well gentlemen, we will take it slow the first couple of weeks; our test subjects showed clear evidence of heightened abilities in the third week. So, the plan is to step things up in week three, but Tory we will have plenty of blood and tissue samples for you all to study." Raphael noticed that Houston was staring off in the distance. "Excuse me Houston but you seem to be preoccupied with something else, do we need to have this conversation at another time?" "No Dr. Springer, I am listening, I believe we should run the project exactly according to the schedule you developed. I will not be here for most of the program so just keep me updated on the progress." Tory shocked at that last statement grabs Houston by his arm. He could feel his blood begin to boil. To keep from making a scene he flashed a quick smile then spoke to Houston with a clinched jaw.

"This project has been our focal point for the past five years, what could come up to take you away from this."

"'Tory, I have business in Arizona I will be back as soon as I can. Is that okay with you?"

"Hell no! I really don't feel your heart is in this program, so you are running to hide in your Arizona compound. The one our government would love to know its location. I should share that little information with the general."

"Tory please don't question my dedication to this project, I am here and will be here for the duration." Houston turns to walk away but turns back to say, "Raphael please keep me in the loop. Tory I will be in constant contact with you." Houston exited the room. Tory leaned in close to Raphael and whispered, "you run everything you are reporting to Houston through me first." Raphael was beginning to feel pressure from what seems to be a situation brewing between her two cohorts. "Tory, we have never operated like this, we have always had open communication with one another."

"That is true, but Houston has never acted this way, I don't know what he is up to and until I do he will get the information I want him to know." Raphael started shaking her head like she didn't want to hear that. "Tory you are being just a little paranoid now!" The shocked look on Tory's face surprised Raphael. "Yeah, doc maybe it is just me being paranoid, I just want this project to work."

"Tory, so do we. We are all in this together!"

"I hear you doc it just doesn't feel like that right now; excuse me I need to make a few phone calls." Tory pulled out his cell phone as he walked to the door. He was feeling uneasy about the actions of Houston. He wanted some assurance about the future of this program. Once he exited the room, he put his phone up and pulled out a burner phone. There were two contacts listed on the phone, Ace and Red.

He punched the contact Red, and the phone began to ring. The video screen lit up when it was answered but you could not make out the figure on the other end, just a dark silhouette. A deep raspy voice answered with a simple "Yeah?"

"I need to place an order."

"Go ahead with your order."

"I need some landscaping done at Raphael Springers address; her information is in the profile I left with you." Tory could hear the shuffling of papers in the background. The raspy voice answered him. "We will have your order ready in 24 hours just remember we don't deliver without full payment."

"That is not a problem." Tory hung up the phone and looked back through the door window at Raphael. His thought, this is not right but I have to do this to keep everything under control. She glanced back at him and waved, he flashed a fake smile and waved back, then turned and walked down the corridor.

Six weeks later:

Tory and General McClain were in the back of a jeep speeding across the compound. "Ok Tory why do you have me out here about to die in this damn jeep?"

"Sir we wanted to give you a live update on the project."

"Really you brought me out here to show me another mediocre discovery, did the weekly emails that reveal no progress become too much for you?"

"Not this time sir, we were taking things slowly with volunteers, but today is their second major training exercise. The result of the first training exercise is why I called you." Tory leans forward to tell the driver speed up we are running late.

The General interrupted that conversation with a question he was dying to ask just to see Tory's response. "Tory, you said we, then where in the world is Houston?" Tory would not make eye contact with the General, he took a deep breath before he answered his question. "Houston had to travel for business." The general gave Tory a surprised look. "Business huh?" That business must be very important, since he will miss the so call fruits of your group's labor?"

"Trust me sir we will have plenty more displays like this." The jeep abruptly comes to a screeching halt. Tory and the General quickly walk into the observation building. The ten-floor elevator ride was in complete silence. The elevator opened to reveal a large room with several large monitors along the walls to their left and right. Directly in front of them were six workstations equipped with multiple monitors that displayed body cameras along with human vitals in real time. There were six people standing around the workstation in an engrossing conversation or debate. In front of the workstation where a wall should be, were large glass windows that stretched from the celling to the floor.

Outside of the windows was the Prototype program training ground; it looked like a section of the rainforest was cut out and deposited on the base. The training area was approximately 4 miles in size. The conversation was silenced when a soldier shouted officer on the deck. The men and women snapped to attention; the General walked past the workstation directly to the windows and grunted out "At ease." "Someone tell me what in the hell I am looking at, because all I see is greenery." Tory walked up with a pair of HD6 glasses and handed them to the General. "Sir to our left you can see two of our top volunteers in the project, Elise and Chris. They have been given task of navigating through this field in 30 minutes and capturing that flag to your right."

"That does not seem that difficult."

"That is true sir, but we have the members of Seal team 12 tasked with capturing those two."

"Well okay now, that is one of our most dangerous Seal teams. They are well known for their ability to camouflage and eliminate targets in silence, this should be good. This will be entertaining for me to see 12 in action, this will probably be bad for your program. Has 12 entered the field yet?"

"Yes they were there before Elise and Chris entered."

"I don't see them."

"That is where the glasses come in; they allow us to see through the trees." The General tries on the glasses; it takes a moment for his eyes to adjust. Once his eyes adjusted, he could clearly see the soldiers. "Ok now I see them, but are they using camouflage?"

"Yes sir, they are, this whole area is designed where these glasses and our cameras view it in 3D; so, we get to see everything clearly."

Just one more question, do the two volunteers have these glasses?"

"No sir they do not."

"Are you sure?" The general responded while pointing out a location on the field. Tory looks out to see Elise perched in a tree very still while Chris moves through the brush. The General blurts out "It is no way that she can see those men, no way." Tory turns to the staff and shouts. "Put twelves communication on the intercom." The intercom comes to life with voices whispering. "Sargent, I have movement at my nine o'clock; I need a green light to punch his ticket."

"There are two bogies, are you only seeing one of them?"

"I have movement on one and he is getting closer, he is moving really fast." The sergeant asked in his comm link. "Does anyone have eyes on the second one?" There was no answer. The twelve like to use stealth to their advantage so they only talk on their coms when it is absolutely necessary.

So, silence meant no one had seen Elise. Sargent had an uneasy feeling about this test, usually his team has had time to prepare for their targets by studying them to find and attack their weaknesses. Today they were thrown into this drill with very little information on their targets. Their instructions were to track and apprehend two individuals with special abilities. Nothing felt right about this, the reputation of the 12 was on the line. They were supposed to be the aggressors, why was the target moving toward them? Even though this operation was not like their normal, the group always performed well in live events. They go over as many scenarios as possible before the actual engagement. They even refer to each other by numbers during an operation. They practice this so that anyone listening to their communications would still have trouble figuring out their locations and who was moving where. The sergeant is the only one in the group not referred to by a number. Because the group is known as the Notorious 12, no one in the group is called the number 12, so he is referred to as sergeant or sarge. Right now, the sergeant could feel his heart beating in his ear drums. This was training no live ammunition just stun weapons. He felt in his gut that his boys were about to deal with something special. He whispered into the com link. "Ok 4 and 6 flank the moving target, 8 you are green lit, punch that ticket when it shows. Everyone else find our second target now." His men began to move carefully and slowly through the brush trying not to make any noise or obvious movement. Things went silent for the sergeant. Operating in silence was normal for this group, but this silence was for far too long. The sergeant mumbled to himself; I should have heard a shot by now. He whispered into his com link "8 have you punched that ticket yet?"

"No sir, I lost him."

"What! How?"

"We started moving and he stopped."

"Did he see our movement?"

"Not sure Sarge."

The sergeant then moved to a higher vantage point unable to spot anything, he again whispered into the comm link. "4 and 6 do you have an eye on either of the targets?" Their response was dead air. "4 and 6 come in." The sergeant pulls the test issued sidearm from his holster and blurted out into the communications. "Men take evasive maneuvers we have bandits in the nest!" Just then the sound of firearms erupted breaking the silence.

"The Sargent shouted someone report what is happening?" His men were continuously firing their issued test weapons. "What the hell are you shooting at? Report now!!" From the skybox Tory and the General witnessed an amazing feat. Chris and Elise were each armed with only a taser baton. They both entered the terrain simultaneously at the north end of the site; then quickly moved into range of the soldiers. Elise took cover in a tree, while Chris drew the attention of the soldiers by moving toward them. He suddenly stopped moving when two of the soldiers flanked him on his left and right. Then it happened. Chris quickly and quietly climbed up into a tree, and then launched himself toward the soldier to his left. The soldier the crew referred to as 4 never saw him coming. Chris landed directly in front of the soldier; the soldier tried to raise his stun weapon to fire, but before he could Chris gave him a quick punch to his solar plexus, knocking the wind out of him. Chris then pinned the weapon to the soldiers left shoulder with his right hand and cracked his right jaw with his elbow. The soldier dropped to his knees. Chris tapped him on the forehead with his stun baton knocking him out. This took all of 30 seconds. Number 6 saw some movement in the brush where number 4 was located. He started to creep toward the movement ready to open fire. He got a glimpse of his fellow comrade on his knees. He then saw a black flash, then the sky. The black flash was Chris's baton flying through the air and dropping number 6. The General and Tory did not know if the soldier fell from the stun from the baton or the sheer force that it was thrown with. At this time three more of the soldiers unknowingly moved into proximity of Elise responding to the commotions they were hearing. Before number 6 body hit the ground, Elise sprang into action. She dropped out of a tree on to number 3's shoulders stunning him with her baton at the base of his neck. As she rode his limp body to the ground, with a flick of her wrist she launched her baton at number 1 with the same results that Chris had. Elise lay still on the terrain floor while number 1's body fell to the ground. The thud his body made caught number 9's attention so he moved in that direction. He slowly pushed through the brush to see the muzzle of a gun aimed at him.

No chance to react, Elise squeezed off two quick rounds dropping number 9 where he stood with stun bullets. The remaining soldiers reacted to the sound of Elise shot, with shots of their own. The chatter on their comm links returned with number 8. "We have two bandits on the southwest edge cornered. I am sure I got one of them with my shots." Number 5 quickly responded. "Okay 8 we are headed your way now. Do you have eyes on any of the bandits?" 8 started his answer. "Negative I....." All of a sudden, he notices to his left, Chris crouched down in front of a tree with one of his comrade's rifles. He tried to spin and get a shot off at Chris, but he was too slow. When Chris saw one body part move, he squeezed off three quick stun rounds. Number 8 finished his spin and fell face down in the brush. Tory and the General witnessed Chris and Elise armed with the weapons of the soldiers they subdued. Pick off four the remaining five soldiers one by one, at an unbelievable pace. The Sargent of the 12, hearing the shots get closer to his location decided to move their flag to a spot he could secure alone.

He quickly moved further south away from the gun fire. He didn't care how much noise he made moving through the brush. He wanted a secure place to draw these two out and accomplish his team's mission. He found a clearing that led to what looked like the face of a cliff. He could hear movement behind him, no time to climb safely; he placed his back against the rock and took aim at the brush in front of him. The only way to get this flag was to come straight for him. He could hear the brush moving to his right; it may be a decoy, so he continues to survey the entire opening for movement. He was ready to unload on whichever one of them popped out. This was only an exercise, but he could feel the intensity in this moment. The brush movement grew stronger; no time to wait this distraction ends now. He let off six quick bursts from his stun gun in that direction. The movement stopped, then the body of number 2 falls out of the brush. The Sarge was surprised to see one of his men emerge from the brush. "What the hell" .... he then saw movement out of the corner of his right eye. He slowly turns to see Elise holding the flag and Chris aiming a weapon at him. He drops his weapon and raises his hands in surrender. "You two took down my crew that fast, what the hell are you, robots?"

Elise smiled and said. "GAME OVER!" Then Chris squeezes off two stun rounds into the Sergeants chest. General McClain looked at the running clock timing the exercise. It was no longer moving and was flashing 15:10. "Fifteen minutes! They took down twelve navy seals and crossed a 4-mile terrain in fifteen minutes!" He grabbed Tory by his face with both hands. "Tory, are you telling me the entire groups of volunteers are like this?" Tory hesitated before he answered, "well sir, these two are our best, the remainder of the group is at about half of their potential."

Elise Wells and Chris Thompson were both 5-star athletes before joining the Army. Elise was a basketball and track star in Mobil Alabama while Chris was a football and baseball star in Memphis Tennessee. They both excelled at any and everything they attempted, from the classroom to field. They entered the military at the same time and after a few years of service they learned of one another. They were the two cadets making the news moving through the military ranks at a phenomenal pace. They finally met in Georgia during their Special Forces training. It was clearly evident that there was a strong attraction between these two all-star soldiers. They flirted with the attraction for years, but when they found one another at the Prototype testing center they decided to explore the relationship. The relationship quickly evolved into a deep love. They enjoyed two things, each other's company and making everyone look bad in the Prototype program including the instructors. Tory and his group quickly realized the potential of the program with the right candidates. Elise and Chris were proving to be the shining example of this.

~❖~

Tory noticed a huge smile on the Generals face, then completely out of character he felt his vice grip hands on both shoulders. Tory has never seen General McClain this close to someone. McClain shouted "my dear boy you have secured all of the funding you will ever need for the Prototype Program. Download the results of this exercise to a secure device; Vice President Mason will be very interested in this." The General released Tory, whipped out his phone and sent out a quick text, while Tory downloaded and encrypted the data from the exercise. As he reached out to hand the storage device to the General, he asked, "sir are you sure about the funding?" The General let out a hearty laugh grabbing the unit; he turned and started walking toward the door. He blurted out "who the hell is taking me to the front gate?" One of the privates jumped out of his seat, "that will be me sir." They walked out of the door with the General checking his phone.

Tory feeling uneasy, repeated his question this time loud enough for the entire room to hear. "Our funding General are you sure, about what you just said?!" The General stops at the door and smiles.

"Check your Dager bank account I am sure you will be pleasantly surprised." The General made his exit.

7 months later.

Doctor Springer sat in her office watching her tablet analyze information about the two soldiers laying in her sick ward. These were the two best that the US had to offer, and she knew that if they died, there would be a lot of questions. Suddenly there was a knock at the door. Raphael mumbled "come in." The door swung open, and Houston entered the room. "Hello doc, I have not seen you in a few days how have you been?" "Hey Houston, I am stressed how are you?" Houston chuckled at that statement and responded, "about the same."

"Houston, I just can't understand why we are having so many problems with this project. These men and women are the equivalent of superheroes, but they are still getting severely injured during routine training exercises." Houston lets out a long sigh; "yeah that is puzzling. So, I got your message you said we needed to talk immediately." Just then the monitors to his left caught his eye. "Hey, you have someone in the sick ward?"

"Yes, we are just running some test on a couple of our volunteers." She quickly answered trying to get his focus off the monitors to avoid more awkward questions. "When I left that message Houston, I was just frustrated it felt like the walls were closing in on me. I just wanted to know what other options I had with this progra…" Just then a notification alarm went off on her tablet grabbing both of their attention. Houston read it aloud. "Pregnant Elise Powell!" He then jumped up from his seat and stepped to her window, the window looked down onto the medical wards floor. He snatched the curtains back to see Elise Powell and Chris Tolbert lying in beds with tubes and wires going everywhere. "Doc, why in the hell are two of our best soldiers in the med ward and I was not notified?!!!"

"Now Houston, please calm down. I can explain this!" Instead of listening, Houston snatches open the door that led down to the medical ward. The stairwell was dimly lit and very narrow.

He hurriedly made his way down the stairs taking two at a time; with Doctor Springer following bracing herself with the walls to prevent from falling. Houston entered the ward and took Elise chart from one of the nurses while she was in the process of making notes. Raphael stumbled through the doorway with all eyes in the room on her. She now regrets wearing those high heels she loved so much; she may have sprung both ankles running down the stairs in them. She leans back against the wall trying to catch her breath; her heart was beating so fast it felt like it would jump out of her chest. Houston cleared his throat, "ladies please give us the room." Houston then slowly turned toward Dr. Raphael dropping the chart to the floor. He began walking toward her. "They are dying; our two best soldiers are dying!"

"No Houston, not just these two, all of our soldiers are dying."

"What!" Houston shouted. Raphael began to slowly walk toward Houston looking down at her feet.

"I discovered about six weeks ago that the PEG delivery system we are using to administer the Prototype serum has been attacking the soldier's organs." She finally makes eye contact with Houston, nowt standing directly in front of him. "All of our volunteers are on borrowed time." Houston turns to look at Elise and Chris in their beds. "All this time we have been using this delivery system. Why wasn't it stopped?"

"Well, I reported my findings to Tory over two weeks ago."

"So that's why Tory, wanted to unearth our old nanite program Hollinger1009."

"I guess so Houston, he swore that he would be able to reverse the affects. He wanted to get a handle on this before bringing you in on it."

"How many doc?"

"How many what." Raphael quickly responded. Houston then repeated his question sternly.

"HOW MANY?!"

Raphael picked up a stack of charts and handed them to Houston. "Five have died, the five accidents during training were actually staged."

"So, you all lied, those five all died from complications? How long do these two have?"

"Right now, I honestly don't know."

"Has Tory been able to reverse any of the affects?"

"He has had some promising results with his work; it just has not been completely effective."

"The two of you kept me in the dark about something as important as this. Why?"

Raphael responds with tears in her eyes, "Houston, please believe me I wanted to tell you. Tory had me in a bind and would not let me say a thing about this."

"So, this is what that message on my voice mail is about?"

"Yes, I just could not carry this secret any longer."

"Does Tory know that you reached out to me?"

"No, I don't believe he does, he was there when I left the message for you. I told him I would not tell you, but neither of us expected to see you on the compound any time soon."

"Okay doc, are these two healthy enough to travel?"

Raphael's voice cracks due to her nerves. "Wait what? What do you mean travel, where are they going?" "Doc right now, you are in no position to ask questions. So, again are these two soldiers stable enough to travel?"

"It is possible to transport them, but they will both need close monitoring."

Houston lowered the tone of his voice as he walked toward Raphael; "okay doc this is what will happen. A Paullina Lopez will come see you. She will need to be completely updated on the health of Elise and Chris, as well as the methods of treatment you have been administering. Did Tory give you a copy of our nanite program?"

"Yeah he did, but it is not the complete version. I just assumed that he didn't completely trust me."

"That does not surprise me with Tory. Do you have any of the nanites accessible?"

"Yes sir!" Raphael quickly responded. "I have six chambers of them in my office. I wanted to run some of my own test with them."

"Great, now a Nicole Mason will be with Paulina. She will need a copy of the Hollinger1009 program, including any updates Tory has made. She will also need at least four of the nanite chambers. Finally, and most importantly, you will cooperate with my people without questions are we clear?"

"One last thing doc, when it comes to Tory. You and I never spoke about any of this. I am still in the dark on what's been going on here." Raphael felt like the air was sucked out of the room. She just nodded in agreement with Houston. Houston taps a button on his earpiece and starts talking as he exited the room. Raphael could not here what he was saying but his body language as he briskly left conveyed that he was really upset.

Feeling pretty low, Raphael gave instructions to her staff to prepare the patients for travel; then slowly walked back up the stairs to her office. She takes a deep breath, as she stared at her silhouette reflected from the dark screen on her tablet. Her thoughts drifted to how she got into this predicament. The opportunity to work with Houston was the main reason she chose this project. Now she has disappointed the brilliant scientist she looked up to. "How can I fix this; how will I ever regain his trust?" Raphael mumbled with tears in her eyes ………. Suddenly she was startled back to reality by a loud knock at her door.

Raphael knocked over a cup of coffee on her desk. She quickly reached for her tablet and papers to save them from the liquid as the door swung open. There stood a petite young red-haired girl with a backpack on her shoulder. "Woah, now that is a mess! Are you doctor Raphael Springer?" She asked with a snarky tone. Raphael now very agitated shouted "who the hell are you?"

"Whoa, whoa doc no need for all that attitude; Houston sent me I am Nicole."

"Nicole," Raphael repeated with a puzzled look. "You are here already?"

"Yes, we are already here duh. Houston said that you would be expecting me."

"I was, but not this soon. I thought you would be here in a few days."

"Nope we are here right now! I believe you have something for me?"

"Oh, my goodness, you have to excuse me I am a little frazzled right now you startled me. Can you give me a minute to collect myself?

"Nope, time is money, and we are on a tight schedule. Just point me in the right direction and I will be out of your hair in a second."

"Well ok, the chambers are in the fridge at the back of the room." She then reached into the desk top drawer and pulled out a data drive. "Here the nanite program is on this." Nicole grabs the tablet sitting on Raphael's desk and turns it on. The tablet looked like a thin piece of light grey glass when deactivated; but when activated it displayed images in 3D. "I will not share my login information with you! We do have security protocols around here."

"No worries doc you don't have too." Nicole quickly responded as she pulled a similar tablet out of her backpack and connected the data drive to both tablets. Raphael sits up in her chair with a surprised look on her face. "How can you possibly know my..." Nicole holds up her hand to stop Raphael in mid-sentence. "Yo Squirt, get in here!" A skinny young man enters the room. "Yeah Nicole, I am right here no need to yell, what's up?"

"In that large fridge in the back of the room, grab four of the blue chambers and we will be out of here!" She said glancing back down at the tablets. The young man looks at Raphael from head to toe and smiles. He then grabs a metal case from Nicole's backpack and walks quickly to the fridge.

"Sorry about that, now what were you saying doc?" Nicole said looking up from her tablet.

"How are you able to log in on my device and how do you know what the program is called to manage the nanites?" "Unless you already know all about the program?"

"Gold star doc, we have a really good idea of the program since it is based on Houston's and Tory's old work."

"It is Nicole right?"

"Yes doc that is correct!"

"Nicole, are you cloning my entire tablet?"

"Kind of." Nicole said with a smirk.

"What the hell do you mean kind of? I have some very important and highly confidential information on that tablet!"

"Oh Please, your private files are not our concern. The short answer to your question is I am not just copying your tablet; I am copying all your devices. Houston really wants to see exactly what you have been up to." "Hey Squirt, are you finished?" Nicole shouts while she is unplugging her equipment.

"Will you stop yelling I am right here waiting for you." He responded standing behind her at the door. Raphael stood their motionless shocked by what she just heard. She racked her brain trying to remember what incriminating information could be on her devices. Her thought process was broken by Squirt's voice. "By the look of your face, it looks like someone was using company material for personal use. I wonder what we will find?" Nicole makes her way to the door. "Let's go Squirt, oh and doc don't leave town any time soon, I am certain Houston will be back in touch with you." The two walked out of her office discussing what type of juicy information was on her devices. Just as the door closes Raphael's office virtual intercom chirped. An image of a nurse dressed in blue scrubs appears in the center of the room. "Doctor Springer."

"Yes, go ahead nurse."

"There is a lady here asking for you. A miss uhh, excuse me but what is your name again? Miss?!" The nurse yelled looking away from the camera. "Dr. Springer you need to get down here, these people are here to take our patients away." Doctor Springer was now feeling overwhelmed, and it was showing. Throwing her head back she lets out a deep breath. "Okay, I am on my way down." The treatment center doors flew open to reveal a frustrated Dr. Springer. "Now what!? Who in the world are you?" There stood a lady with long flowing black hair down to her shoulders. Dressed in fatigues with a white lab coat, an outfit that is normally unflattering for a woman, but Raphael noticed that was not the case for her. Even in that outfit she commanded the attention of the room. Her dark brown eyes locked in on Raphael. "Hello Doctor Springer, I have heard so much about you, it is a pleasure to meet you. I am Paullina Lopez; I work with Houston. He did say you would be expecting me."

Raphael stood eye to eye with a beautiful dark-haired woman. Raphael forced a smile, then reached out to shake the young lady's hand. "The pleasure is all mines Paullina. Houston did not waste any time in getting you all here. At least you are more polite than the group that was in my office." Paulina smiled and shook her head. "I take it you met Nicole and Squirt; they are known for leaving a lasting impression."

"Boy that is true!"

"Houston notified us a week ago to be ready for something like this.

"Wait, really a week ago?!"

"Listen Raphael, woman to woman, Houston has always had a feeling some things here have just not been right."

"This is him making sure none of this comes back to bite him. Trust me if he has to, he will destroy both you and Tory." Raphael dropped her head when she heard that. "I never meant for things to become so complicated."

"I hear that, but you have to understand that Houston considers deception as one of the greatest betrayals."

Raphael mumbled with her head down "I just cannot phantom how I allowed this to happen to me." Paulina took both of Raphael hands and whispered to her. "Only one thing can explain that; and that one thing is Doctor Tory Drew. He should be in the hall of fame for his manipulation of people."

"That is so true Paulina, and I knew that going in that is why this sucks so badly." Penelope broke the awkward silence from Raphael statements with a question. "So, doctor what else do I need to know about these two patients?"

"What else?"

"Yes, what is not included in their files?"

"Well for one the female is around four months pregnant."

Paulina took a step back, "okay that is interesting but the look on your face says there is more?"

Raphael final makes eye contact with Paulina and responds. "Well, she is pregnant with triplets."

"Triplets oh my that is a twist. How are the babies doing?"

"They are all healthy for now, the question is how healthy can you keep Elise their mother. Paulina, let me ask you a question; because from my experience in dealing with these men and women when they become ill, they go downhill fast, and I mean really fast."

"So, Raphael was that a question or a statement?"

"Well, no but my question Paulina is how in the world will you all be able to get up to speed on Tory's nano program; correct it and implement it before these two expire?"

"Raphael, I told you Houston notified us a week ago to be ready to move patients from here. We have been preparing for the last four months to treat them." Raphael was completely shocked by that statement. She responded in disbelief. "Wait the last four months, what in the world is going on?"

"My dear Raphael, nothing is ever as it seems with the US Government. The Hollinger program was one of Houston and Tory's first groundbreaking military technologies. Back then the program was used to infiltrate the mainframes for satellites, weapons, aircraft you name it. Houston knew some pharmaceutical companies paid Tory a truck load of money to turn the program into a new miracle treatment. So, Houston started working on that treatment also. Houston never knew exactly what you two were up to out here, but he knew when his old friend dusted off the Hollinger1009 program it was time for him to step in." Paulina takes Raphael by the hand and leads her outside of the treatment center. They were standing shoulder to shoulder right outside of the door. She had a clear view of what was going on inside and outside of the med bay. She began whispering to Raphael. "Word is the Government has always been spying on Tory and Houston. I was not supposed to divulge this to you, but I have a feeling you are telling the truth. You just got caught in a bad place; so, I will leave this with you. The upper brass is sending some investigators to question everyone here. My advice to you is to forget you ever saw us." Raphael froze with panic. "Wait investigate who, us!?"

"This can't be true; how much trouble am I in? Is this a criminal investigation?" Paulina, placing one finger over her lips, and gave a simple, "Shhhhhh remember you don't know any of this." Then she just turns and walks away without any more answers. Raphael reenters the med lab and dismisses the nurses in the room. She began to walk back to her office. Her head was now really spinning; military brass asking questions, her career, the possibility of prison. Now her stomach was churning. She reached her office and bolted straight for the restroom. She spent the next 45 minutes on her knees puking her guts out. She laid there on the cool porcelain floor in a puddle of her own tears. She could feel the fear now setting in, she never thought that her actions with this project could take such a horrible turn. The bathroom door slowly opened. As she wiped fresh tears from her eyes they focused on the figure in the door. It was Houston. He ran some cool water over a towel then he placed the towel around the back of her neck. "Do you think you can pull it together long enough for me to give you some instructions?"

"Instructions on what Houston?"

"On what to say too the Governments goon squad when they arrive. Hopefully we can keep you out of serious trouble."

"Will your instructions keep me out of prison or just buy time so that your people can escape with those bodies."

"To save time and avoid a debate, let's just go with both." Houston sternly replied. He helped Raphael off the floor and led her to the couch in her office.

"Houston I am so sorry for all of this, if there....."

Houston cut her off. "Listen save the apologies for now." He sat her on the couch and then took a seat in her chair. "Okay I will go through this once quickly because we don't have much time. You try to wait for them to reveal what they know about the project."

"Why wait?"

"Well don't you think it will be good to find out what type of charges they will be bringing against this program? Regardless of that your answer to them will be this; everything you did here was because you were in fear for your life. Provide the investigators this jump drive; tell them you discovered the information on Tory's tablet."

"What is on the drive?"

"Information about Tory's offers from Pfizer and Bristol Myers to upgrade the Holllinger1009 program into a wonder treatment for brain injuries and Alzheimer that they could market to the public."

"Houston I...."

"Don't try to explain yourself anymore; just do as I say and maybe we can keep you out of prison. The drive also reveals that Tory had information on you he was using it to force you to participate in all of this. The deaths, the cover up and the use of neuro toxin treatment on the soldiers to manipulate them."

"So that was a mean mind controlling agent he administered, and he claimed he said he would never use that on these men and women."

"Welcome to the real-world Raphael, Tory was not just carrying out military orders. When problems began to arise in the program, he decided the only way to succeed was to create an army of elite soldiers to do his bidding. He accomplished just that with some of them."

"Oh God, what in the world is his bidding?"

"You name it world power, control the normal psycho philosophy. You were going to be his helper in developing his program then become the crazy military doctor that receives all the blame for what went wrong here. One good thing for you is he doesn't know that this is coming. This gives you a chance to get ahead of the story. Provide them with this information and then leave if they will let you."

"Leave and go where, I can't go home."

"Just go somewhere Tory can't find you! This will really piss him off and put you in line to see his narcissistic personality."

Raphael looks up at Houston. "What about you? The information of what has been going on here will make us both wanted by the government."

"That is true doc, but they will not be able to find me. Tory on the other hand will not go down without a fight. One more thing, make sure you let them know that you have been seeing black trucks outside your home and office and you believe your communications devices have been compromised."

"Houston I don't know if I can pull this off, everything I tell them will be verified by the investigators." Just then her office door swings open and in walks Nicole. Nicole drops a new cell phone that looked like a smaller version of her tablet in front of her. "Have you been out there the whole time?" Raphael said standing to her feet.

Nicole smiled and gave a very sarcastic response, "what will really rattle your cage is whether or not I ever left."

Houston shaking his head at Nicole brings Raphael focus back to their conversation. "Now Raphael on this device Nicole brought in, you have at least 20 photos of surveillance trucks outside your home and this office. Your home is bugged, and this cell has been forced paired which detects where you travel at all times. All of this leads back to Tory and his people. Either play the game the way I have instructed or face the possibility of being tried under the Patriot Act. We know how that could potentially end; the choice is yours." Houston made eye contact with Nicole to stop her from talking. Houston takes a deep breath "Raphael this is one of my associates Nicole."

"Yes we met earlier." Nicole interrupts the conversation speaking in an impatient tone. "Houston our meter is running out, it is time for us to disappear." Houston rose from the desk with his eyes focused on Raphael. The stress of the past few hours was beginning to show on her face. He tried to hide his emotions, but he knew what was coming for her had the potential to be very bad. He had to continue to remind himself that she and Tory were setting him up to take the fall for this. Well, if she must be the sacrificial lamb that allows his group to disappear then so be it. Raphael stood there looking at her feet, feeling so alone her hands were visibly shaking as she picked up her new phone. Houston now standing at the door felt compelled to say something. "You can get through this doc, just continue to play the helpless victim role, you do that so well." Fighting back tears Raphael responded in a high pitch tone,

"now Houston that is not fair for you to say that"

"Raphael, just stop with the drama and play your part. If all this gets too hot for you there is a contact in your phone named Sabrina Rhodes. Tell the authorities that you want a lawyer and call her!"

Houston turned and walked away without looking back. He could not deny the feelings he had for Raphael; he and his team had done all they could to help her. Now all he can do is pray that she does not disappear. Raphael sat in her chair alone in silence for at least an hour, as her mind began to turn against her. She could only imagine this going sideways, being held in the basement of the pentagon inside one of those interrogation rooms that does not exist. She could feel her blood pressure rising, not feeling well, she decides to go home and try to get some sleep. As soon as she arrived at her home, she took two sleeping pills, chased them down with a large glass of wine, trying to silence her thoughts. She just laid back on her couch staring at the celling. Raphael was awakened by the morning light shining through the skylight in her den. She glanced at her phone and the clock read 0915, she felt a little better with some rest but now she must face this day. She slinked into the restroom to get ready. Raphael arrived at the base at 1030 AM, while gathering her things from her car she noticed several black SUVs with tinted windows parked in front of the building. Where these people here for her? She takes a deep breath and slowly exhales, "okay let's get this over!" Raphael turns and heads for the door. She could see her favorite guard Carl on his normal post at the front desk. She knew something was not right as soon as she entered the door. Carl who was normally jovial and flirtatious with her, hardly made eye contact. Raphael decided to approach this like a normal day. She blurted out "good morning Carl, did you shrink your shirt or have been working out? Either way it looks good." Carl gave a reluctant smile and replied very dryly" good morning Mrs. Springer." Raphael stops at the console to scan her identification and she hears "Mrs. Springer?"

"Carl, since when are we so formal?" She scanned her badge and an alert appeared on the screen to detain. Carl stood up and responded with a strong tone. "I am being formal today because we have company." Just then two men in black suits step forward.

"Mrs. Springer, "Carl said dropping his head. "I have to ask you to go with these men please."

"Ok Carl," she responded as she turned and walked toward the men. "Mrs. Springer your id badge please," said one of the young men dressed in a black suit, white shirt, and black tie. Raphael nervously handed her badge to the man. "Now Mrs. Springer if you would please just follow me to the conference room."

"Who is in the conference room?" Her question was answered with complete silence. She followed the black suits for a short walk as they turned down the hallway about 20 meters from the buildings front entrance. There was a side entrance to the main conference room located on the first floor. Another man in a black suit was there waiting with the door open. Raphael entered the room to hear. "Great she is here now we can get started; Mrs. Springer this way please, take a seat here." Raphael walked slowly through the door into the large conference room. Expecting to see a room full of US military brass, she was astonished to see two women and two men in dark suits along with General Hast. The young man that was standing at the door pulled out a seat and placed it directly across the table from the General. "Mrs. Springer have a seat." As she sat down the young man then sat down next to her and began typing information on a tablet. Sitting down slowly Raphael took a long look at the General. He had to be to be in his late fifties; he had a large round face with wrinkles. His hair mustache and beard were snow white. He was a very large man who stood 6 feet 6 inches and a body that looked as if it was carved out of stone. His presence in the room seemed to be five times larger than his size. He sat down across from her biting down on a half-smoked cigar; his deep dark eyes seem to pear into her soul. His hair said he was no longer actively participating in field maneuvers, but his body screamed he was built just for hand-to-hand combat. Raphael cleared her throat. "Who exactly are you guys; I have never seen military personnel dressed in all black. Are you all the men in black?" She smiled hoping to lighten the mood. That floated like a led balloon; the response was complete silence. General hast was still staring directly at her. She dropped her head in fear expecting to hear a booming voice come from this large man, but she was startled as a blond-haired lady sitting to the Generals left spoke up. "We hear that all the time, just so you know we are called team Apollo, and Mrs. Springer we are hoping you would share some information with us." Raphael smiled, "share some information with you? Outside of the General I have no idea of who you all are; I believe you have the wrong person here." Raphael stood up, and General Hast spoke in a very low monotone voice, "please Mrs. Springer have a seat, you are exactly who we are here to see. We are here to gather information about the project your DAGER group is working on in this building."

"Again, sir I repeat I do not know who you all are; plus, our work is highly classified, and you do not have the proper clearance to speak about it!" The young blond lady quickly responded, "who we are is not your concern. We have clearance for all things related to United States especially this little Prototype program!" The General leaned back in his chair as he crossed his arms over his chest and shook his head at Raphael as if she was a toddler. "No, we are here for the use of the Hollinger1009 program, and the possible cover up of soldier deaths in this program. So, let's do it this way to prevent you from wasting our time with the I was in fear for my life, or I am completely innocent role. We ask you a question you give us a direct answer and maybe you will continue to see the sun each day." Raphael dropped back into her seat as if she was hit in the chest with a ton of bricks. The young man that was sitting next to her was now standing over her. "Your phone and tablet please Mrs. Springer." She reached down for her bag to retrieve the items and he just abruptly takes the whole bag. The blond speaks up again, "ok Mrs. Springer let's try this again, when was the last time you saw Tory or Houston?"

"I believe it has been about two weeks since I have seen or spoken with either of them."

"Two weeks is that normal?"

"Yes, they like for us to have time to present large amounts of data based on our test for them to review."

"Wasn't Houston here yesterday?"

"I am not sure; they both have the highest clearance on the base so they can come and go without any of the staff knowing."

"That may be true, but you are not just staff, your name goes on the findings along with theirs; and you're telling us, he was here and didn't speak with you?"

"Like I said General, I did not know he was here I was focused on my work; I guess we missed one another." Raphael responded with frustration.

"So, Mrs. Springer what is Hollinger1009?" The blond blurted out. That question startled Raphael; she could only wonder what all they knew about her. "Well, I am not completely sure what it is; I just know it was a personal project of Tory and Houston."

"Have you administered it to any of the participants in the Prototype program?"

"I believe Tory did." The General piped in with a booming voice. "She didn't ask about Tory she asked did you!?"

Startled by that outburst Raphael responded with a shaky voice. "Knowingly, no I did not administer it." The General leans forward in his chair, his eyes were now burning a whole into Raphael's head. "Knowingly, now that is a curious word. Your job description on this project was to manage the health of the participant's, right?"

"That is correct sir."

"Then Mrs. Springer how is it that you don't know anything about Hollinger1009 when it has been responsible for several of the participant's deaths?" Raphael had to take a deep breath, she could feel the walls closing in on her again, she tried to continue with their story. "Well sir we have had soldiers killed in training exercises, but none to this Hollinger1009 that you are speaking about." The older bald headed white male sitting to the Generals far right immediately stood up dropping a thick file onto the table directly in front of the General. He began to pat the folder in front of him as he slowly spoke. "Mrs. Springer, I believe the correct way to describe this is that the Prototype project is using training exercises accidents to cover up participants deaths due to the use of Hollinger1009." Raphael felt a lump in her throat as she tried to swallow. She looked directly at the general "sir do I need a lawyer?"

The bald-headed man to his right sarcastically responded, "do you, need a lawyer?"

"I need my phone, please sir."

The General blurted out with his hand extended, "Rick her phone!"

"Yes sir," the slim young man gave her tablet and phone back to her. "They are both clean sir no damming information on either. Her phone has normal text messages between her and both scientists; nothing there for us. Oh, and I was able to detect that her phone has been cloned. I used an algorithm to triangulate the phone running the program. It traced back to Tory's last known location."

"Private was he listening in on this meeting?" The General asked with serious concern.

"He may have picked up a little, but I was able to jam his signal." The bald man in the black suit leans into the General, "sir in my opinion this was just a little too convenient for us to trace this back to Tory. This seems like a planted excuse for her." The General smiled, "Mrs. Springer did you know your phone was being monitored?" Raphael was done answering their questions. "Excuse me sir but I need to make a call."

"That will not happen; we don't want you alerting either one of these scientists."

"I just need to get a number out of the phone General."

"This interview is just getting started what makes you think we are going to allow you to contact someone outside of this room!"

"It's simple sir, the only person that I am talking to from here on out is my lawyer."

"Mrs. Springer," the General stood up and began walking toward her, "we are not here to charge you with any crimes."

"Not yet!" The blond blurted out. The General raised his hand to stop her mid-sentence. He then took a seat on the table to Raphael's left and placed his hand on her shoulder. "Listen we are simply here to gather information of what actually went on. We are here to help you. In all actuality the people in this room are the only ones that can help you; not someone in this phone," he said while waving her phone inches from her face. Raphael looks down for a few seconds, the realization that she could become an enemy of the state, and one thing she knew as an enemy no one in our government would help her including the people in this room. Trying not to panic Raphael said at the top of her voice; "I will take my chances with my people, my phone please!" The General chuckles while looking back at his group. "OK," he held out the phone for her, but snatched it back when she reached for it. He then slides the conference room phone across the table to her and hits the speaker button.

"Make your call on this phone, so we can ensure you are not calling your coworkers."

"Ok, that's fine I just need to get the number." He hands her the cell phone while watching her every move. She quickly scrolls through her contact list then franticly dials 10 digits on the conference room phone.

There was a pause before the phone began rigging. Two rings, then a third, she started to sweat as she thought, did Houston set me up? She noticed everyone in the room had a victory smirk on their face. Four rings, then five, she thought to herself, oh God help me please. Then she heard a voice say, "state your name?"

"Excuse me I am trying to reach.." The voice gets louder cutting her off mid-sentence.

"Yes, ma'am I know who you are trying to reach, state your name please this number is not registered in our database."

Raphael could hear snickering in the room, and someone sad under their breath. "Did she dial 1 800 get a lawyer," the snickering turned into laughter. Raphael looked directly at the four black suits still laughing, as she spoke. "My name is Raphael Springer alpha six tango forty-five."

"Hold please." The line goes silent for a couple of minutes which felt like a lifetime to Raphael. She sat there with her head in her hands fighting back tears. Suddenly the female voice breaks the silence. "Okay Mrs. Springer please hold for Sabrina Rhodes." The room fell silent; she looked around there were no more smiles in the room. They were all replaced with very serious looks. It was clearly apparent that whoever this Sabrina was, her reputation obviously precedes her. "Mrs. Springer, Sabrina here how can I help?"

"Well, I believe I am in some trouble."

"Stop, are we on a speaker phone? Pick up the receiver please."

"Mrs. Rhodes!"

"General Hast I should have known that this was your handy work."

"I cannot allow Mrs. Springer to speak to you without us being able to hear the discussion."

"Even you know that is a violation of this young lady's rights. Now Mrs. Springer will you pick up the receiver."

The General places his hand on the receiver. "Well Mrs. Rhodes if we go in this direction, we will have to charge Mrs. Springer under the Patriot Act. Which basically means we get to do what we want too." The phone went silent for a few seconds; then Sabrina responded. "Raphael I am headed to you, do not say another word to anyone until I get there. Not another word, General Hast you will be sorry for this."

General Hast grabbed the receiver and hung up the phone. He and his group all exit the room without saying a word. Raphael sat in that conference room for at least two hours before the thin blond lady walked in to check on her. Feeling frustrated Raphael shouted, "what is going on why are you keeping me in here." The young lady exits without an answer. Finally General hast and his crew reenter the room and the General shouts "take her into custody!"

"Wait, why are you taking me into custody sir?"

"We will see if some time in a confined space will make you more cooperative in answering our questions."

"General everything that you have done here has been against my legal rights; this needs to stop now." General Hast cleared his throat before answering. "Mrs. Springer, your government answers to our branch, the only rights you have here are the ones that I give you. Now stand up!" Just then the conference room door flew open and a slim figure, in a black dress walked into the room. She was barely 5'2" in her heels but to Raphael she was 8 feet tall. Her salt and pepper short cut hair accented her skin which was flawless. The room fell silent until she spoke, and her voice screamed control and authority. "Your branch may run the Government, but I run the men and women you answer too. I told you over the phone to leave my client alone; but I get here to find you handcuffing her. Take those off now because Mrs. Springer is leaving with me. From this moment on Hast, you only question my client with me present, or spend the rest of your career washing Government vehicles." General hast looks at Raphael with a serious scowl; he then turns to face Sabrina.

"It is such a pleasure to see you again Sabrina."

"You may want to hold on to those sentiments, because until all this nonsense that you are stirring up gets settled. You will not like me!" Raphael collected her things and moved to stand behind Sabrina, like she was a barrier between her and the General's group. Sabrina scanned the room then turned to Raphael, smiled, and said, "let's go darling they have nothing for us here." The two exited the room and headed down the hallway for the front entrance. Raphael turned to see if they were being followed, surprisingly there was no one there. She started to breathe a sigh of relief as they exited the building, only to see the General standing on the stairs having an intense phone conversation. She knew right then that all of this was not over. Raphael hurried to get into Sabrina's car, but as soon as both of their doors closed a military police car swooped in with breaks screeching to block her Audi Q35 from exiting. Sabrina showed her frustration as she leaned on her horn. "They cannot keep us from leaving." Sabrina yelled as she leaned on her car horn again. Raphael looked at her in disbelief.

"Sabrina, I have been around these people for a very long time, and they can, and will do what they want, to whomever they choose."

"They don't do this with me;" she leaned on her horn for a third time. Just then there was a knock at Sabrina's window that startled the women; it was the General. She hit the button to automatically let her window down, while staring directly at him, in disgust. "Tell your flunkies to move so that we can leave!"

"Now Sabrina, we have soldiers being manipulated into participating in off the books testing with mind altering drugs. Some of those same soldiers were killed in mysterious training exercises, and the one person we can find connected to all of this is sitting in the passenger seat of your truck. The top brass wants answers for this; somebody must be held responsible. In other words, Sabrina you are free to leave but not your passenger." The General gives them both a huge smile. "Your passenger is staying here with me." He then steps back from the truck, straightens his jacket, then signals to the MP car with a head nod. The General then starts to whistle as he turns and starts walking back to the front door. At that very moment four

MP's exit the vehicle blocking Sabrina's car. To her amazement one of the MP's had a device that unlocked her vehicle. They forcefully removed Raphael from the vehicle. Sabrina bolts out of the driver's side door and around the rear of the car to see Raphael on her knees in tears being handcuffed. Her hair was out of place from the scuffle, covering half of her face. Sabrina could clearly see the distress in her eyes. Sabrina was not expecting this, she was knocked off her game. Before she could say anything to the MP's, General hast steps in front of her. "Now don't you go and obstruct justice. She will be charged for her crimes and after she has been processed then you can speak with her as her legal counsel."

"General this is a bunch of bull, what are her charges?"

"Just stay tune Sabrina, we will inform you."

"What the hell does stay tune mean? You will tell me what my client is being charged for now. This is not legal."

The General got uncomfortably close to Sabrina's face. "Do you see the fence surrounding this compound? Outside of it is your world, inside is ours, welcome to our world! Now you are free to leave, and we will be in touch."

Sabrina moves in closer to the Generals face. "I will not leave until I have a chance to meet with my client! Understand me General once I clear Raphael, my next mission will be to end your career!" She pulls her cell phone out of her purse. "General make my request happen soon or my world will engulf your world like never before!"

The General lets out a hearty laugh and sarcastically responds, "good luck with all that!" He then begins walking up the stairs. Sabrina turns her back to him and begins a conversation on her cell phone. General Hast headed directly to the young blond woman standing next to the front entrance doors. "General, we were able to get a trace on the attorney's phone. She is speaking with him now!"

"Just as I suspected; Sabrina wants to know what we know."

"We should be able to get a location on Houston in a moment."

"Great, have that conversation recorded and dispatch a team to his location. I doubt if any of this works, but it is worth a try. Let's keep Raphael on ice for now, she is proving to be more valuable than I thought, maybe she will force Houston to poke his head out and we can then pounce on him. Then we will have all three of them in custody." The General turns to the parking lot to see Sabrina still on the phone.

"Houston, it is General Hast who is running this operation. He clearly will break every law in dealing with Mrs. Springer to bring you out of hiding."

"Well, if that is the case Sabrina then let's give him what he wants."

"Are you sure about that?" Sabrina said looking back at the general. "He has not made it clear why he wants you and Tory so bad."

"I am sure it has something to do with pushing his team's agenda; just take care of Mrs. Springer the best you can, we are on the way." Sabrina hangs up her phone and walks up the stairs to where Hast and his people were. "Excuse me sir, but I will be waiting to see my client once she has been processed." The General opens the door for her, "by all means please come in." Sabrina walks through the door and turns to the General, "so all of this is all about Houston Creed?"

"Listen the Government wants him and Tory by any means, I am just following orders."

"So, the Government sent their prized hunting dog to entrap all these people. We all know the only orders you follow are the ones that benefit you and your team. You will not entangle my client and destroy her life with your political witch hunt." The General abruptly stops walking, stares into space for an uncomfortable amount of time. He then turns to face Sabrina. Looking down at her, like she was his 18-year-old daughter. "Sabrina, for the last time, we have soldiers who lost their lives due to this little experiment. We are here to bring justice to every person that had a hand in this crime; from your client to Houston and Tory and anyone else, including you."

"Me!?" Sabrina shouted in shock.

"Anyone that had a hand or knowledge of this crime will be prosecuted under the Patriot Act. So yes, even you! Now if you will excuse me, I have some things that need my attention. We will let you know when your client is ready for you. One last thing, the next time you speak with Houston let him know his time has run out, it's best that he turns himself in."

"General I believe you are being a little presumptuous." The General gives a huge smile as he eases in closer to Sabrina, and he whispers. "With the information we have, this is not presumptuous it is the tip of the spear." Suddenly the Generals cell phone rang, he tapped the screen and a image of the young blond appears. "Sir we have tracked Tory to a laboratory in Queens New York. We have a team there about to breach in two minutes."

"What about Houston Kelly, any location on him?"

"We are still working on that sir."

"I will be up there in a second;"

"Yes sir!" His phone went dark, the General then popped his half-smoked cigar in his mouth turned and walked away without looking back. Sabrina took a seat outside the holding cells; she had a sinking feeling in her stomach that Raphael, Houston and Tory will never get to see the inside of a court room.

This felt like one of those conspiracy stories you hear about the Government making things and people disappear. She let out a huge sigh and mumbled under her breath "I hope Houston has a plan because I don't."

CHAPTER 03

THE PERNICIOUS

The Pernicious originate from a very large planet called Balzen in the Kemet galaxy. They are approximately three thousand separate colonies; all governed by the oldest and largest colony Alpha 13 and their current Queen Dylan. The colonies all functioned together for the betterment of the Pernicious race; survival by all means is the code that they will always live by. They survive by feeding on the life source of other objects and beings. They used the Kemet galaxy as their very own food source; by harvesting and feeding on all the Kemet planets inhabitants except for one plant called Novalucent. Novalucent is a planet on the outer edge of the Kemet Galaxy, about half of the size of the Pernicious planet. It is home to the Novian race and guarded by their Light Warrior military. The Light Warriors were the main reason the Pernicious avoided their planet. They may be smaller in numbers, but they had developed weapons that effectively damage their armor and ships unlike any other being they have encountered. The Pernicious main food source was the second largest planet in their galaxy called Salent. It was home to over 3 trillion inhabitants. For some 500,000 years the Pernicious used Salent and the other planets as their sources for food, until a large asteroid struck Salent. The Pernicious tried their best to harvest as many lives as possible off the planet, but within a year every living organism was dead on Salent. Without their largest source of food, the Pernicious quickly ravaged all the other planets in their solar system. Now that their food source has been severely depleted and billions to feed; the Preeminent Queen Dylan had to decide to leave or watch their species become extinct.

The largest building on Blazen was a dome shaped building that looked as if it was made from golden mirrors. It sat in the shadow of the Alpha 13's nest. This was where the preeminent queen Dylan and her colony reside. "Queen Dylan Things are becoming very desperate around here. Word is spreading that there is not enough life source to sustain our world. What will we do?"

"Yes, my dear Goliah we have been dealt a serious blow. The time has come to rethink our sources for food here in the Balzen quadroon to sustain our race. Our ancestors warned us of this day. Go and have some of our men prepared to scout the planet Novalucent. We will pay them a visit and show them the full fury of the Pernicious. "Goliah, one last thing, have the queens Azieal, Arcia, Yolin, and Jarmier come to me at once.

"Yes, my Preeminent."

The four queens arrive at Azieal's quarters. They were meeting in her very large and impressive rotunda den. The walls were her favorite color of royal blue and adorned with very expensive solid gold decorations. Every five feet along the wall was a 15-foot statue of a guardian in full battle gear. Queen=n Dylan stood in the center of the room at the head of a large clear octagon shaped table. The top of the table is twelve inches thick and looked as if it was carved from an iceberg. Inside of the table were several mummified skulls of known Pernicnious traitors. The anguish of their horrifying death was captured on their faces and amplified by the material the table was made from. The four large support legs were made of granite and the bones from these traitors. Rib cages, hands, feet, and spines were clearly visible in the table's legs. "Come in and sit we have a lot to discuss." Azieal pauses and waits for the other two queens to sit down, to ensure that she was the last to take a seat. While waiting for everyone to sit, she opens the conversation, "Preeminent, we as a clan have never faced anything like this. Will the demise of the mighty Pernicious be your legacy?" Dylan slams both hands on the table speaking at the top of her voice. "Hush with your insubordination Azieal, I did not call you here to hear your opinions! Continue and I will personally harvest and feed your nest to my Guardians." Dylan and Azieal stand at either ends of the table eyes locked on one another not moving. Yolin's voice breaks the growing tension. "Are we here to fight or did you call us here for a reason Dylan?"

The two turn their attention to Yolin as Azieal finally takes a seat. Dylan begins to walk around the table. "As you all know our 5 colonies are the cornerstones of the Pernicious. We have now entered a very unsettling time for our people. I hear the grumblings that we are on the brink of civil war."

"Those are not grumblings you hear Dylan, we will not sit and slowly starve to death and do nothing. Civil war is much closer than you may believe."

Dylan stops pacing around the table to respond. "My young Jarmier understand this, nothing will ever happen here on Blazen without me knowing! We will not starve; my scouts have been sent out to develop an attack plan for Novalucent. Which once it is conquered it will replace Salent as our main source."

Azieal lets out a sigh. "Novalucent, do we really want to open that door again?"

"Azieal this is not a matter of want but need; we need that planet as a source until we find new quadrants."

Azieal responds with the look of utter confusion. "Find new quadrants!?"

"Yes, once we secure this new source to sustain us we will begin sending out scout teams to locate new quadrants with abundant life sources. Blazen will always be our home but now is the time that the entire Universe kneel! What I need from all of you is to maintain peace here between our people." "Maintain peace!" Shouts Arcia; "the five of us are the Pernicious, we should leave this world to the rest of those puny colonies."

"Is that really how you feel about your brethren Arcia?"

"They are not my brethren they are beneath me, sustenance for my colonies survival if I choose!"

"Is this truly how you feel? Is this how all of you feel? Have you all forgotten that our dominance is in our numbers? They are the reason we are who we are now! We are not five colonies looking down on others. We are all one! If we separate, we are no longer the world conquering Pernicious; we are just colonies on borrowed time. Understand me we will always need all of our people to over through Novalucent and every planet in this Universe!"

"Ok Dylan, calm down we all can hear you."

"I don't want you to hear me Jarmier, I want you all to understand. We have and will always be one clan." All four queens answer simultaneously. "Yes, my Preeminent."

"Now that we have that straight, I am trusting that you all will manage the food source and govern our people while I am away. On my return I expect there to be nothing different, if there is any chaos, I will hold you four directly responsible and we all know what that results in." She said while patting the table above one of the mummified skulls. The four queens sat in complete silence as Dylan stood up from the table. "I will also expect you to have everyone ready to invade on my return. Is that clear?"

"Yes, my preeminent!" They all replied. "Now leave me I must prepare for my trip." The four young queens leave Dylan's lair; they were standing outside in the fading sun light and began making plans for the task before them. Arcia shares her plan, a plan that was far more extreme than Yolin and Jarmier and Azieal expected. "Do the three of you really expect Dylan to return here?

"Why wouldn't she?" Jarmier questioned.

"Because she has the coordinates to a brand-new feeding ground; would you come back?"

"She is the preeminent queen she cannot abandon our family. Plus, we all have those coordinates."

"Maybe that is my wishful thinking Jarmier, because either way she will not be the preeminent for long." "Arcia, it sounds like you have plans of something different." Arcia gives a huge smile to the group. "Listen, Dylan's strength is in the size of her colony and her loyal followers. Without the followers, their colony becomes vulnerable." Jarmier responds with excitement in her voice.

"Are you talking about attacking Dylan's colony? Even without her loyal followers, her colony is still very dangerous. Not to speak of what would happen to you if you failed."

"Yes, Jarmier I am aware of the consequences with this, but I am not talking about attacking her more like forcefully convincing her that we are more powerful."

"Arcia, it seems like you have put a lot of thought in this, so just humor me what do we accomplish by convincing her that we are more powerful?"

"We convince her to leave her discovery for the four of us where we begin a new family under the government of our colonies."

"This is treason just standing here talking about this." Azieal responded.

"I know but just hear me out. We first significantly reduce the food sources that we provide to the smaller colonies."

"Okay, but that will not destroy them!"

"That is true Azieal, but within weeks they will all be at war for survival. That will reduce their numbers significantly. Which means Dylan will have to rely on us to succeed during the invasion of Novalucent." "Once we secure the planet, we turn our guns on the smaller colonies eliminating them until there is only Dylan left and we force her to run."

"What if she chooses to fight instead of run?"

"Then Yolin, we will never see her or her clan again." Arcia said with a smirk. The queens begin to slowly walk back to their lairs in complete silence, all three considering the repercussions of this.

The Alpha 13 nest drops out of hyper space about 60,000 miles above the planet Novalucent. Near the moon Zorist; they were familiar with this moon and its inhabitants. On Zorist, there were a small group of beings that the Pernicious named Shadows. They were called that because they were able to alter their appearance becoming invisible. The Pernicious had no way of detecting or tracking these beings so they decided to hunt them down and kill them. Those that they were not able to kill were captured; over time the shadow beings had become extinct. The Pernicious kept a few hundred of them for testing. This was the only being able to escape their detection, and they had to know how. Among those few hundred was one named Zeal who is now a stowaway inside of Alpha 13's nest gathering as much information as possible. The captives knew the Pernicious were becoming weak because of the food source they lost; and he was looking for an opportunity to free his people.

Dylan enters the control room of the Alpha 13 nest. "What is our status?"

"My Queen we have been able to jam all sensors from the planet they are unaware of our presence. Our primary scan of the planet revealed that their military has increased in size since our last visit."

"Their most extensive weaponry is around the Kings palace. It remains to be the most heavily fortified place here."

Dylan shook her head in agreement. "This is what we were expecting, so what is your analysis?"

"Our assumption is, if we take out their heavy weaponry and overtake the palace they will surrender." Dylan walks closer to the screen displaying the Kings palace. "This moment is too important; we need to go on more than just assumptions!" She turns to face her people. "Goliah put together a scout team, take a ship down there and determine if this site will be the focal point our attack."

"Yes, my queen." Goliah gathered 20 soldiers and another guardian to make the trip. Unknown too Goliah was that as they loaded into the clipper ship, they were accompanied by Zeal. Goliah, gives instructions to his pilot. "Okay cloak the ship and circle the area that Alpha 13 transmitted to us. Gather as much information as possible about their weapons, ships, personnel, and defenses. Then land at our designated location."

"Do you believe this will be enough information for us to formulate a formal attack Goliah?"

"Based on the information we have attacking this area will significantly cripple their ability to defend this planet. A bonus will be if their leader is here, and we can force a surrender to save bodies. Either way we will be victorious in another campaign!" The Pernicious clipper ship lands about a mile outside of the Novians military compound. Goliah, Paine, and five solders exit the ship to get a closer look at the compound and determine which building will be the focal point of their attack. Zeal still undetected by the Pernicious also exited the ship with a different purpose.

He was heading into the compound not just to warn the Novians of the coming invasion; but to provide them with all that is known about the Pernicious. His hope was that these beings could use this knowledge to be the first to defeat the Pernicious in war. "My King!"

"Yes Sigma?"

"Our Lieutenant is reporting that they captured an intruder inside of the palace; we are now on high alert."

"How was the intruder able to elude security?"

"That we are still looking into; our guards say he appeared out of thin air outside of the wolf quarters and asked for you by name."

"He made it that close to me!" The king responded with concern. "Sigma, I need to know what his intentions are?" It was clearly obvious that the Novian king was growing impatient.

"Sir, I believe our men are questioning him now." Suddenly one of the guards enters the room interrupting Sigma and King Ai's conversation. "Excuse me my King. The intruder refuses to give any information. He continues to ask to see you. Permission to make our questioning physical?!"

"No, soldier just bring him to me." Sigma interrupts the conversation "What sir? Why would we put you in danger like that?"

"Sigma, we have just as many questions for him as he has for me."

"That's true, but I don't feel that this is safe for you."

"Safe, Sigma he was able to avoid every security precaution we have in place only to stop a few feet away from me and ask our guards to bring him before me. I believe if he wanted to do me harm, he had every opportunity; let's see what this is about."

"Sir, I really don't feel comfortable about this; you will be heavily guarded while he is here."

"That is fine Sigma, let's just get on with this." Sigma returns with Zeal in shackles and 10 armed guards, they stop and stand him in front of King Ai with Sigma standing to Zeal's left as the guards surrounded the three. King Ai looks at Zeal from head to toe focused on his every move. "So who are you, and why are you here asking for me?"

Zeal bows his head to acknowledge the Kings authority. "Sir, I greatly apologize for my intrusion, but I had to ensure that I'd get to speak with you. My name is Zeal. I come from Zorist, one of your moons."

"Okay Zeal, I am King Ai and to your left is my second in command Sigma." Sigma abruptly interrupted. "Enough of the pleasantries how were you able to navigate around our security systems." At that moment the shackles holding Zeal captive fell to the ground as he disappeared reappearing on the other side of Sigma. The guards and Sigma all turn their weapons on Zeal as he raises both hands.

"I have a special ability that enables me to avoid detection or capture." King Ai was really captivated by this. "You are a Naridan Shadow, we believe that to be an old bedtime story to entertain the youth. How many more of you are here?"

"I am here alone to warn you of the imminent danger approaching. It is not me, but the destroyers of worlds you need to be concerned about."

"Who?" The king blurted out looking at the puzzled faces of his men.

"Sire, I am speaking of the Pernicious!"

"Zeal, we know of the virus that has plagued many of the planets in our system. We have tangled horns with them on several occasions, but they have never ventured to our boarders. How do your people know them?"

"Today your people and mine have a common enemy. For the past 15 years my people have been hunted by the thousand to be utilized to train their young in hunting and tracking. They have a fascination for my people because of our unique abilities. Since our first encounter with them, I have been on a crusade to free my people! The Pernicious made the decision to pick up roots and find new systems to prey on and that starts here. Right now, there is a ship on the outskirts of this city as well as a a nest orbiting the planet with one of the moons. This is just the tip of their spear." Sigma quickly walks over to a console in the corner of the room and radios the control center. This is the central nervous system for the palace. "Yes, sir Sigma?"

"Run an scan to see if there are any ships near the city or orbiting above us."

"Sir I am not detecting any ships but there is something interfering with our sensors."

"Switch to our UV scanners!" There was nothing but silence on the other end of the radio. Then King Ai speaks up. "Do you see anything son?"

"Sir you need to see this."

"SEE WHAT?"

"Well sir, we have two signals one outside the capital and something is orbiting one of our moons, whatever it is it is huge, four times larger than the moon."

"Find out what is jamming our sensors and work around it so we can see exactly what you are detecting, I am on my way."

"Yes sir!"

"Sigma you take Zeal and our lieutenants and gather all the information he has about the Pernicious being here. Brief me as soon as you are ready."

King Ai enters the control room. The room was designed like a large command center of an aircraft carrier. Half of the room was equipped with video screens on every inch of the walls. There were several separate acrylic workstations where his men receive and transmit data with drones that were spread out over the entire planet. The center screen in front of the workstations displayed a live look at the Alpha 13 nest orbiting one of the Novalucent moons.

"My king I was not able to figure out how they were jamming our sensors, but I found a way around it, I was able to reconnect with our drones. Sir, we have one of their scout ships in the mountains outside of the city with a scout team that is a little too close to the palace for comfort. Then there is this." He said pointing at the screen in the front of the room. "Sir, that is the largest ship I have ever seen." The King spins to see Sigma and Zeal entering the command center and he shouts.

"Sigma, put our military on high alert for invasion."

"My King, 60 percent of our military is off world."

"Get them back here now! From my understanding of the Pernicious we will have more of those large ships here soon; and they will be doing more than just scouting." One of the soldiers at the communications array turns to the king and Sigma with a concerned look. "My king we are not able to make contact with any of the generals that are off world." Zeal, was captivated by the view from the large window that overlooked the city. The large glass buildings in the many different shapes, sizes, and colors. The buildings went in every direction as far as he could see. He was amazed at how the light reflected off each building in a different color. He was snaped out of his daze when he noticed the military officers racing across the crystal bridges that spiderwebbed over the gallery below. Their haste reminded him of the looming threat. He turns from the window and steps forward King Ai; "it really does not matter how many men you bring back you will only be prolonging the inevitable. You will never have enough fire power to stop their invasion; that is why your planet has been chosen."

"So, are you saying we should lie down, just surrender?"

"No, I am just telling you to be prepared for the worst case because you may be faced with it very soon." "If it comes to that then I will deal with it but for now we will prepare to destroy these so-called world killers!" King Ai shouted. He then turns to his men, "Sigma, were you able to gather anything of worth from our visitor here?"

"Yes my king we have information on their attack formations and strategies. I have already distributed it to the heads of our protective forces to begin formulating a defense. Sire with so many warriors off world we are the only line of defense; if we fall here this whole planet falls." King Ai took a moment to consider his sergeants words.

He stood there staring at the image of the large ship orbiting his planet as if he was frozen. He then breaks the silence in the room with commands. "Sergeant, begin procedures for evacuation of all women and children, contact both of our sister planets to alert them of the forth coming threat and ask them to send weapons and bodies to assist in our defense. And Sigma."

"Yes Sire?"

"I need my ship prepared for Babylon."

"Babylon!? Sire do you believe it will come to that?"

"Sigma, you and I both know we have more than just a planet to loose; we cannot let the origin scrolls fall into the hands of others."

"With all due respect sire you sound as if we have already been defeated before firing one shot."

"Sigma, as King my sole responsibility lies with ensuring that the scrolls containing our secrets remain in our possession, and if it comes to Babylon then so be it. Now if you are through with your line of questioning, carry out my orders!" Sigma looked around the room to see the look of disbelief on the men's faces. His answer to the king was against every fiber in his body. He simply mumbled, "yes my king." King Ai and his Novian soldiers began to feverously prepare for the coming invasion. Goliah's ship returns to Alpha 13's nest and the nest makes the hyper jump home to gather the troops. While Dylan and Alpha 13 were away doing resonances on the planet Novalucent. Arcia, Yolin and Jarmier were launching their plan to change the hierarchy of the Pernicious. The three began by tainting the remainder of the Pernicious food source, leaving the smaller colonies weekend and in dismay.

They then began a campaign to discredit the preeminent queen by telling the other queens they discovered that her plan was to sacrifice their colonies to conquer this new land. Then when the planet is under complete control of the Pernicious, she will turn her warriors and guns against what is left of the smaller colonies. Cleansing the clan of its weakness is what they said she called it. The three young queens' plans were beginning to work. The pernicious hierarchy that the colony relies so heavily upon was becoming very unstable. With Dylan away unable to quench these ru-mmors, they spread like wildfire.

Her betrayal had been put into motion; she returned home not to a planet ready for invasion, but one on the brink of civil war. Dylan immediately calls a round table meeting with the queens she left in charge and their first Guardians.

"I return to a planet in turmoil, on the brink of civil war. What is the meaning of this, why are you acting as if there is no hope for our existence?"

"Dylan we are not in the position to be patient, our colonies are on the brink of death, and we never had clear understanding of your intentions." Arcia quickly responded. Dylan sitting at the head abruptly rises to her feet, slamming both hands on the table. "MY INTENTIONS! My intentions are to secure a new land for this group."

"Or" Arcia again quickly responds, "are your intentions to sacrifice our people to gain victory in your conquest, and then simply turn your guns on the grunts that help you conquer this new land!"

"WHAT! Why would I...." Dylan pauses and turns her attention to her young sovereign Azieal, Yolin and Jarmier. All three avoid making eye contact with her. "Arcia I do not know of this sacrilege you speak of; but I do know we do not have time for this.

Our survival now lies on Novalucent, and it will take every soul on this planet to gain control of that system. So, you all tell me would you rather sit here and debate with me about propaganda while our colonies die?" Dylan pulls a dagger from her belt and slams it into the table the blade sinking half way into the table. The pearl handle adorned with the Pernicious symbol seemed to glow in the light. "Or do we plant our flag in a new land and ensure that the Pernicious civilization will continue to grow and thrive. Arcia sighs aloud, "you may be correct Dylan the survival of our people is what we should be focused on, but all of us here have questions of you that need to be answered." Dylan looks over the room, "I assure each one of you, we can have those conversations once we have control of Novalucent." Dylan then pulls her dagger from the table and lays it down flat resting on the hand guard. She then begins to spin the dagger, "and I also have some questions to be answered by each of you." She then slams her hand on top of the dagger stopping it from spinning the point aimed in the direction of the Arcia; "and be it known an act of treason in any form is a crime punishable by a slow and painful death!" Dylan eyes locked with Arcia. Without breaking eye contact she shouts."Goliah provide their guardians with the intel needed for our mission." She then takes the dagger and runs it down her left hand cutting it. She then balls her fist as her blue blood drops out onto the table. She then smiles at her sovereign queens, "and Goliah sound the horns to let the clan know it is time to prepare for a new blood campaign!" Dylan simply turns walks out of the room without another word to the four ladies. As soon as the conference room door closed behind Dylan; the room erupts in conversation between the queens. The conversation continues as they all began making their way towards the door. Arcia, Yolin and Jarmier leave Azieal and exit the nest through a side entrance. "Arcia she knows!"

"Jarmier we don't know that yet."

"She directed that treason statement to us."

"No Jarmier, she directed that statement to everyone in the room. Plus, a lot of the queens are dismissing the plans we put out and are falling back in line with her. They just need more coaxing that's all."

"What if we can't coax them, I mean what happens the?" Jamier asked with obvious concern in her voice. "What do you mean Jarmier are you no longer with our plan?"

"Arcia this can go very wrong for us if we are not careful."

"We knew going in there were risk, right? Right Jarmier?"

"Yeah but.." Arcia cuts Jamier off "But nothing I tell you what you go and prepare your colony to invade Yolin, Azieal and I will take care of Dylan."

"Yeah Jarmier it is clear you don't have the stomach for this; we will do all the work and you will reap the benefits like always!"

"Yolin that is not fair!"

Arcia stopped walking and express her frustration. "Jamier, just go and prepare your people!" Jarmier pauses before she starts to slowly walk away with her head down. Yolin turns to Arcia "I have an idea. Do you have a loyal subject willing to sacrifice his life for his queen without question?"

"Yes I do!" Arcia said with a sinister smile. "Good, so do I. We will need to get them both onto Dylan's nest before everyone lifts off." Arcia now really intrigued responded "Why her nest?"

"We need a sacrifice to start this Civil War why not use our weak link. We will have our people fire on Jamier's nest from Dylan's." Arcia smiles, "that sounds delicious to me."

Unbeknownst to the Yolin and Arcia, Azieal was tucked behind a column listening to their conversation. As the two began their walk back to their individual nest Azieal quickly makes her way back inside of Dylan's liar. Dylan's servants were dressing her in combat gear when she noticed movement behind her. Looking in her full-length mirror she makes eye contact. "Azieal why are you still here?"

"My queen it is urgent that I speak with you!"

"My young one we do not have much time to prepare, can this wait?"

"No, my queen, the treason you spoke of is true and will be acted on during our invasion." Dylan stops her servants and turns to face Azieal. "How do you know this?"

"I just heard Arcia and Yolin planning to plant soldiers on your nest to launch an attack on Jarmier's nest." Dylan stood still for a few seconds digesting what she just heard before responding. "That plays into the rummors that have been planted and will prompt all of my followers to turn their guns on to my nest in the belief of survival."

"Yes, that seems to be their plan, but I fight with you my queen together we can destroy the three of them right now, before laying siege to Novalucent."

"Right now, I do not believe I can trust the four of you. How do I know this information is not a part of the treason plot? All four of you want your chance at the preeminent throne." Aziel felt those words like a punch in the gut. She dropped her head before responding. "My queen I understand how you feel, to be completely honest I have had reservations about your decisions lately; but I am Pernicious to the bone. I will always fall inline that is how I was raised. I will give my life and the life of all my people for the preeminent throne!"

"Well, it pleases me to hear you say this Azieal, I will alert my Guardians to be on the lookout. Capturing Novalucent will always be our primary objective, and for that we will need all our weapons. What happens after that will be dealt with then. Now go and prepare our people for our new blood campaign!" Azieal quickly responded "Yes my queen!" Dylan stops her before she could exit. "Azieal, one last thing. If you meant what you said about your loyalty to my throne; then I need something from you. Azieal, if something should happen to me, I need for you to ensure that we are victorious in this battle."

"Dylan my queen just let me take care of those three; I have a feeling that this will not end until one of them has risen to take your throne!" Dylan walked up to Azieal placing both hands on the side of her face. "My young one the only thing that matters right now is our campaign, after that you are free to do what you want. My hope after this you will be right where you were meant to be."

"Where is that my queen?" Dylan smiles, "at my right hand! Now go and prepare for greatness; it is time to introduce the people of Novalucent to the Pernicious way."

~❖~

On the planet Novalucent

King Ai walks into the nerve center of his military head-quarters to see his loyal warriors moving around as if they were on fire. "Sigma, what is the problem?"

"Sire several ships just dropped out of hyper space and are heading directly for us."

"What is several three, four? How many ships are there?"

"Sire right now we are not sure!" Sigma stopped to make eye contact with the king. "It is more than four, there are too many to count!" King Ai makes his way to the front of the room where the giant projector screens were. "Bring them up on screen." The screen lit up with what looked like thousands of ships entering the Novalucent atmosphere. One of the sergeants looks up from his desk with panic in his face, "they are back this soon!"

"Sargent pull it together!" King Ai shouted. "Now let's handle this judiciously. Have we completed evacuation yet?"

"No sire we are about 40% complete." One of the men shouted from behind the king. "Then sound the alert for invasion, and Sigma I need you in place right now." Sigma gave a puzzled look before responding, "but Sire, there has not been a shot fired yet!" A clearly frustrated king turned to respond.

"First Sigma, we will soon be fighting for our very own survival, and we must be prepared for everything. Second and most importantly, this is not a discussion that was an order. Do not question me again!" Sigma bows in forgive-ness; King Ai turns his attention back to the room. "Now someone give me a count on how many invaders we have coming and what type of weaponry we are facing!" A fema-le soldier responded from a workstation in the front of the room. She never looks away from her monitor. "Sire based on our projections these ships have the capacity to carry 5 to 7 thousand fighter ships and over 10 thousand soldiers. Our sensors indicate that those large ships have begun powering up their weapons; their first wave of attack will probably be to disable our land to air weapons. Opening the door for them to get their troops on the ground. Sire if that happens, they will outnumber our men by the hundreds; we will not stand a chance."

"Silence that!" King Ai yelled at the top of his voice. "We are Novian Light Warriors we do not entertain doubt! If they invade like a swarm of insects, then we will exterminate them like insects. These aliens will never possess this land, even if the cost is all our lives." One of the soldier's leaps to his feet. "Sire the evacuating ships are returning, they have been taking fire from the Pernicious ships!" Sigma was standing in the doorway listening to what they were facing when out of nowhere Zeal appears. "Your King has the look of concern, Sigma?" Sigma spins around with a shocked look on his face. "Zeal why are you still here? I thought you were being evacuated." Zeal shook his head from side to side, "nope, it was Novian women and children first. We both know I was never going to make it off of this planet. So, it looks like the Pernicious are back?" Sigma frowned at those words like they were painful to hear. "Yeah and they brought more than we expected." Zeal let out a slight chuckle, "they always do, that is how they operate. Their sheer numbers and highly advanced weaponry make them an insurmountable foe." Sigma shot Zeal a mean look. "Insurmountable, not for us, if they breathe then they can and will be killed." One of the sergeant's voices from inside the room captured Sigma's attention again. "Sire what should we do with the people on the evacuating ships that are returning?"

"Have them moved into shelters for protection; and sergeant raise our defense shields."

"Yes Sire." King Ai walks over to the entrance where Sigma and Zeal were standing. "You're still here?" Sigma drops his head to answer his king. "Sire I was just getting information from Zeal, I am headed to carry out your orders now." King Ai nods his head in agreement before speaking. "Sigma, before you leave let me ask, you have tangled with the Perniscious before right?"

"Yes Sire, but not on this scale. Those were very small-scale battles, that happened when we bumped heads with them in the wrong places." The king paused for a moment staring off in the distance, before responding. "I am just trying to figure out what type of attack strategy they are using. Who fires at evacuating ships just to force them to land; why not just blow the defenseless ships out of the sky?" Zeal intervenes in the conversation. "That's because they don't just want this planet, they want your people also; you are their crops. They do not plan to destroy you they are here to harvest you. You didn't believe me?" The king looks at Zeal with uncertainty written on his face. "Now we do believe you Zeal!" He turns to his second in command, "Sigma, are we ready?" Sigma tried his best to look stoic in his response. "Yes sire." Zeal could see that he was struggling with carrying out his orders. King Ai placed his hands on Sigma's shoulders looking him directly in his eyes, "then go and activate Babylon now, and I will give you further instructions soon; and take Zeal with you. He may be of some value in you surviving all of this." Sigma just turns and walks away without saying a word as Zeal follows. "So, Sigma what is Babylon? What does it do?" Sigma now walking at a very fast pace, didn't turn to acknowledge Zeal he just shouted. "That's not your business, now keep up." Zeal noticed that everyone they saw was also moving at a brisk pace. The Novalucent's were clearly in an unusual position being invaded. This made him uneasy, was he wrong in his assumption that Novalucent could put a stop to the Pernicious. Did he risk his life for nothing, he needed answers so he continued to pry for them with Sigma. "Do you guys have a secret weapon for them?" Sigma ignored Zeal's question as the two climbed into a jumper pod. They both strapped into their seats, then suddenly Sigma grabs

Zeal by the throat with his right hand, slightly choking him. Sigma spoke in a tone slightly above a growl, "for the remainder of this trip you cannot talk, or I will personally deliver you to those damn Pernicious myself." Zeal gasped for breath once he released him and sank deeper into his seat. The pod takes off at breakneck speed, as the building rooftops zipped by. They traveled about 100 miles from the base into a mountain region. Zeal notices a huge entrance at the foot of a mountain; Sigma slowed their speed as they flew directly into the dark entrance; the pod pauses for a couple of seconds. The cavern was pitch black, there was zero visibility. Then out of nowhere the pod begins a descent straight down, at unbelievable speed. Unable to see anything Zeal braced himself for impact, he just knew they were going to smack a wall at any time.

As the pod continued to pick up speed, he noticed ahead of them that lights began coming on illuminating the tunnel for the ship. The tunnel began to level off from its steep decline as Sigma slowed the pod down to a stop. Zeal never felt Sigma land the pod, the doors just suddenly opened and the two of them stepped out. Zeal now finally getting his bearings, realized that they were on a glass helipad. He could see the large room directly beneath them. The room was a scaled down version of the control room they were just in with King Ai and his men. Sigma went down the stairs to the room, as he entered the doorway a voice greeted him, "Ident code Sigma, welcome what can I do for you." Sigma responded to the voice, "Isis run a preliminary set up for Babylon." There was silence for a few seconds before the voice responded, "Sigma, set up is complete, please insert activation key and enter authorization code to proceed." Sigma retrieves a silver object from his necklace; he inserts the object into a small board, and it begins to slowly turn; while it was turning, he enters a six-digit code on the keypad. Zeal felt like this was a time to get some answers to his burning questions. "So, Sigma is this place Babylon?" Zeal asked with an inquisitive tone. Sigma let's out a deep sigh and answers without looking up. 'Babylon is not a place." Zeal gave a surprised look, and kept probing, "then what is it?" Sigma looks up from the workstation and answers him with an aggravated tone, "let's just hope you never find out!" He looks back down and continued pecking away on a computer keyboard while Zeal walked around examining the instrumentation in the room. Sigma looks up from the screen to find out where Zeal was. "Don't touch anything!" He looks down and presses a yellow button; Isis voice responded. "Controls are now with King Ai." Sigma opens a communication channel with the master command room. "Sire!"

"Yes Sigma?"

"Babylon is now online; I pushed her controls to your ident bracelet. How are things there?"

"The Pernicious have assumed attack positions and they are using some technology that is causing our instruments to malfunction. We are preparing to take the fight to them before they get more attackers on the ground." Sigma quickly responds, "then I will be back there to assist in the battle."

"No Sigma I need you there, prep the A1668 for takeoff and ensure that our cargo is safe; I will see you shortly." Sigma walks away from Zeal to conceal their conversation. "Sire we can defeat these beings and you need my assistance; I can't just sit here and wait in a freaking cave while a battle goes on above me." The king was clearly attempting to hide the anxiety written on his face, he began to speak in a low monotone voice, "Sigma, right now I need my second in command to just follow my instructions." He paused for a few seconds, staring directly into his communications camera, so that those words would resonate with Sigma. Then he abruptly ends the transmission without saying another word. The king then briskly walks into the middle of the control tower facing the screen with the images of the pernicious ships getting closer. "Private see if you can make contact with them." The private franticly works on connecting with the invaders, before looking up at the king with despair. "Sire they are not responding." The King shouts in response, "keep trying them!" The private stuttered in response to him, "nnno nno sire, I meant they blocked all communications from us." The king was now growing irritated, he shouts out more orders. "Okay men this is what we have been preparing for. Lieutenant open fire on their ships to slow their descent." "Yes Sire!" The Novians ion cannons across the planet unleashed a barrage of missiles directed at the pernicious ships; only to see most of them explode harmlessly against their shields.

The officers stood shocked with amazement at this; the lieutenant now looking for answers from his king spoke up. "I don't understand this, our light ion cannons are able to penetrate all shields. Our missiles are not delivering the damage we were expecting. Could they have new technology for our weapons?" One of the privates shouted as an alarm began to sound. "Sire our shields are coming down!" The king slammed his fist into one of the workstations out of frustration. This war was just beginning, and they were already behind against their invaders. He turned and shouted, "get our damn shields back up now!" The private froze. The king shouted again, "private! Private do you hear me?!" With a somber look the private responded, "sire, I can't, we have lost all control of our systems." The king glanced back at the video screens, then turned to his men. All of them frozen in awe of what was happening to them. King Ai broke the silence, "our story in history will not be about defeat but about the fearless warriors who overcame an impossible threat. Lieutenant get our vipers air born now!" The lieutenant turned to the soldiers manning one of the communication stations and began blurting out orders for them to follow. Comm links all over the planet chirped to life with a voice stressing, "launch all vipers immediately." At that very moment, the pernicious ships opened fire with a coordinated strike on the Novian launch pads. Explosions erupted all over the planet, the tower that housed King Ai's command center shook violently with the explosions. "Private give me a damage report, and somebody in this room get back control of our systems and our damn shields!"

"Sire they are firing at our ion cannons and our launch pads." The king took a deep breath, "How much damage?!"

"Sire, 65% of our ion cannons are now inoperable and we were only able to get half of our vipers lifted off. They will not have any place to land. All our command centers have taken heavy damage; they are targeting our most vital areas." Another private interrupts the conversation shouting. "Sire they just released their fighter ships and landing crafts. There are thousands of them, our ships are severely outnumbered." Ten of the Pernicious landing crafts touch down not far from the tower. One of the lieutenants stepped forward, "sire we are detecting nine to ten thousand Pernicious foot soldiers headed directly for this tower; it is time to move you to a more secure location." King Ai stood motionless in the middle of the command room; the look of grave concern had fallen on his face. They were severely outnumbered; their weaponry and technology were no match for this onslaught from the Pernicious. It has come to a decision that only he could make, destroy a planet and eliminate their adversaries to ensure their civilization carries on; or watch his men fight in vain, and see his people enslaved by these beings. This was the decision he never wanted to make. The officers were now growing impatient, the lieutenant repeated, "sire we need to move you now!" King Ai snatched his arm away from the lieutenant and boldly stated. "I am not going anywhere!" His lieutenant walked up to him, so the room could not hear his words. "But Sire, we have almost lost complete control of this fight; if they capture you this battle is over." The king stepped back and spoke so the entire room could hear him. "It is obvious why they are sending troops here, to capture me. There will be no capture here today. This is our land, and we keep it, or we all die defending it! Lieutenants alert our men to engage the enemy on all fronts; give them everything we have!" The room erupts with cheers as the men began passing out weapons. The lieutenant bows to the king, "thank you for reminding me who we are! Sire it is my honor to fight for Novalucent!!" The lieutenant grabs his weapon and races out of the room. The lieutenants voice could be heard as he ran down the hallway screaming the command to fight to the death. King Ai still standing in the same place looked at the remaining 5 privates left in the room. "Why are you still here?" "We are here to stand with you sire."

"Good then bring me my weapon and get me a way to communicate with Sigma." A loud chirp came from one of the privates personal communications device. He could see Sigma and Zeal on the screen. He quickly took the device to his king. "Sire, Sigma has found a way to reach us!" The king answered, "Sigma I was just about to reach out to you." Sigma ignored that statement and quickly tried to gather some information. "Sire what is going on there? Are you ok?" The king mustard up a small smile, "we are fine, but we have reached the point where I need you to take the A1668 to our sister planet Restall. I will meet you there and we will make further plans." Based on his kings facial expression, Sigma understood that this was the end of everything he knew as a Novian. The King will not meet him on Restall he is planning on destroying their planet to save the secrets of their society. Sigma gives a lifeless answer. "Yes, sire I will wait for you there." King Ai began to speak but, between the communication signal breaking up, and a brutal battle going on in the background; Sigma was not able to make out what he said. "Sire come again I could not make that out." The silence from the other end seemed to last forever; then King Ai voice came through shouting. "Sigma it is time, you know what to do!" Just then the power and communications both went out. "Sigma threw his communication device against the wall in frustration, Zeal had to take cover from the shattered pieces that went everywhere. Sigma then grabbed Zeal by the arm and pulled him toward the launch pad. "it is time to go!" They boarded the A1668 ship in haste. As the voice from Isis blurted out, "the Babylon countdown has now commenced." "Ok Zeal, strap in we don't have much time!" Sigma entered the ships launch code; Zeal could see the Babylon countdown clock in the middle of the ships console. The clock was moving like it was stuck on fast forward. Based on the speed that Sigma was moving getting the ship ready for launch, it was clear that he did not want to be here when the clock reaches zero. He could feel his heartbeat start to race watching the countdown. Suddenly Sigma punched a red button, and both of their bodies were snatched back into their seats from the force of the ship's takeoff. The ship explodes out of the mountain top moving at great speeds. Sigma was still able to look out and see the devastation caused by the Pernicious. He could see his people being captured in droves, and the chief tower had been overthrown, his heart dropped. Sigma mumbled under his breath, "they were more than we could handle." Zeal gave a very remorseful response, "I am so sorry for your loss, but at full strength they are more than any planet can handle, that is why they have existed for so long." Just then a couple of explosions happened near their ship. Sigma turned off the auto pilot and began flying the ship. "We are taking fire I need to get us clear."

"They want live bodies not dead ones; they are just trying to damage the ship so we cannot get away." Zeal responded. Sigma was franticly using every instrument in the ship to evade their combatants' weapons. "I've got the shields up and that should give us enough time to get clear of their weapons." Zeal quickly responded, "The shields wont.." Before he could finish that sentence bullets from one of the Pernicious nests sliced through the A1668 thrusters killing the ships drive. Sigma shouted, "where the hell did that come from?" "The sensors didn't detect that we were being targeted." Zeal leaned forward in his seat with his eyes gapped wide, "Sigma I believe it came from that huge black and grey nest to our starboard side." As Sigma looked in that direction, they both froze in place. A shadow slowly covered their ship. Now directly in front of them was a nest that looked to be 100 stories tall of connected jet-black termite mounds trimmed with gold accents. The huge nest dwarfed their ship, and the gold trim on the ship glimmered from the light of their plasma cannons every time they fired. Zeal gulped as he swallowed, this was the first time that he was able to see the ship he stowed away in. "No doubt those rounds came from that nest; it looks like they are opening their bay doors. Sigma we need to move before we are caught in their tractor beam!" Sigma threw his hands up in disgust, "I've lost all thrust, we are a dead stick." Zeal quickly unstraps from his chair, "Can we repair it? Is there a work around?!" Sigma gave a confused look, "repair thrusters in the middle of a fire fight, that's not an option!" At that instant, blinding light appeared between the ships. A hyperspace portal opened, and the Horizon exited moving at full speed. Sigma and Zeal both covered their eyes from the bright light created by the Horizon's arrival. "Now what in the world is this?!" Zeal shouted still covering his eyes from the light. Sigma quickly scanned the odd-looking ship before it moved out of range, "Zeal, that ship is not Pernicious!" "Then who the hell are they showing up in the middle of a battle; that is beyond being lost!" Sigma was still using the ships sensor to get more answers about the ship, "my sensors can't tell much just that they are from the planet Gaea." Zeal gave a puzzled look, "that explains why they dropped in the middle of a fire fight, only an antiquated system like theirs would have issues with hyperspace portal navigation. Unless they did it on purpose?" Sigma gave Zeal a long-puzzled stare, "that I don't know but you can ask them once we get aboard."

"What!? Wait Sigma, are you hailing them!?" Zeal shouted in disbelief. "Yes!" Sigma quickly responded without looking away from the controls of the ship. "What if they are just as bad as the Pernicious?"

Sigma stopped what he was doing to look at Zeal. "Right now, I'll take that risk. I'm sending them a distress signal to come get us and warn them about the Pernicious impending attack. Hopefully, they will see us as friendly and be willing to help." Zeal sat up in his seat. "I hope you are correct, and that these primitive beings can avoid the impending doom."

Aboard the Horizon

"Tory, we are receiving a distress signal from that damaged ship straight ahead." Tory turns his attention to the screen showing the ship, clearly venting some type of liquid into space. "Can you translate the message?"

"No need, the message is in English." Tory now clearly interested in this event responded, "what are they saying?"

"They are asking for us to bring them aboard, and that we need to leave this galaxy as soon as possible, something about a planet ending event." Tory moved closer to the video display of the damaged ship. "That ship along with this one will give me leverage over our government. Quickly, pull them into bay 5 and send a security team armed to the teeth to great them." One of the men listening interrupted Tory. "This battle is getting intense, and several of those ships have scanned ours! We don't have time to pick up damaged vessels, we need to exit right now!" Tory gives a look of disgust to that question. "Make the time to carry out my order!" He turns to the men behind him "Chris, I need you to plot a course for home, and make the jump as soon as we get that ship aboard." The men in the room looked at one another in confusion. Tory broke the silence, "yes we are picking up aliens and an alien spacecraft. The faster you do that the faster we leave!" The room erupted with activity.

Aboard Queen Azieal's nest one of her navigators gives a report. "My queen the ship that just dropped out of hyperspace is not of this world."

"Are there any life forms on board?" She quickly responds. "Yes but they are not of Novian decent."

"This could be our good fortunes; they represent a new system for us to conquer." The navigator responded, "Queen Dylan has already begun to move in on this rogue ship." Azieal let out a long sigh, "contact her now!" Her eyes flared with fury "and divert a fleet of our vipers away from the battle to capture that rouge ship before she does."

"Yes my Queen." The Navigator began shouting out instructions into his communicator. Just then Azieal heard Dylan's voice sounding very irritated. "What is it Azieal?" The preeminent queens 3d hologram image appeared directly in front of Azieal. "Preeminent, I am sending some of my Vipers to capture the ship that dropped out of hyper space; that way both of our nest can remain engaged in this battle." Dylan snaped a response, "no Azieal, call your men back to the battle now, we are closer and will capture that ship!" Azieal gave a puzzled look, "yes, but Preeminent have you not noticed that Arcia, Yolin and Jarmier nests are now flanking your position?" Dylan stood from her command chair, as Aziels voice echoed in the center. "Yes, I am aware, that they are targeting us, but I have something very special in store for those three. Concentrate your assault on the opposing Novian ground forces; there will be plenty of time for you to assist in what follows!" Aziel smiles in response, "yes my preeminent!" She closed her communication channel with Dylan and barked out orders. "Bring up images of the Novian ground forces!" The screens in her command chamber went black then suddenly displayed images outside of the palace were plumes of black smoke billowed with Novian soldiers ruining in all directions. "you heard our queen open fire on those soldiers until nothing moves!" Azieal's nest unleashed another barrage on the ground forces, that proved to be the breaking point for the Novian military. When they stopped, there was no sign of Novian resistance outside the palace. Thousands of Pernicious foot soldiers took this opportunity to storm the building. King Ai stood in the control tower facing the entrance doors with his 5 guards, listening to the battles in the corridor right outside. "Men if any get through we will make their deaths quick and painful!" The corridor fell silent from the weapons firing, explosions, and screams. "My King, it sounds like the lieutenant and his men were able to hold them off." Suddenly the doors that normally slide open and close were snatched off their frames into the corridor. Crashing metal against stone and glass breaking were the only sounds in the corridor. That was followed by a few moments of silence, eerie silence. The men protecting king Ai, tightened their grips on their guns waiting to open fire. The silence had everyone uneasy, the king could feel a lump in his throat. Was something out there? Then a tidal wave of pernicious soldiers stormed into the room. The king's guards could only fire 5 or 6 shots before being overwhelmed. The king never flinched; despite being surrounded by aliens as far as the eye could see. The group in front of him parted and a large alien with tentacles coming out of his wrist walked forward. One of the tentacles began wrapping around king Ai's upper body, pinning his arms to his side like a vice grip. Then he broke the silence addressing King Ai. "We taught you and your people fear and defeat in a matter of moments; you should have just surrendered." Ai was struggling to speak with his chest being squeezed, "You have taught us nothing! We will never surrender too you!" King Ai raised both arms from his elbows, grabbing the bracelet on his left arm with his right hand and quickly punching three buttons with his fingers. The guardian had up to six tentacles around the King's body by this point. As the tentacles became increasingly tight, the King squirmed and twisted a portion of the bracelet. He whispered with blood streaming from his mouth. "Know that on this day your people were destroyed by the hands of Novians!" The guardian realizing, he just activated something immediately crushed the life out of the king with his tentacles and then threw the dead body out of the window for all to see. The guardian opened a channel on his communications array with the Preeminent nest. His image appeared in front of Queen Dylan's throne. "My queen I have eliminated this planets leader, but he was able to activate some type of weapon!"

"Yes, Atella, we noticed it; it appears to be a very powerful weapon. Prepare to have your men teleported back now!" Babylon was not a weapon in the sense of military weaponry, it was a last line of defense for the Novians if all else fails. The secrets kept on Novalucent were too important to be allowed to fall into the wrong hands. The Novians built Babylon to ensure that this would never happen. It is designed to fire a warhead loaded with antimatter into the planets core. The result would be an explosion equivalent to a one hundred-million-ton atomic bomb; that would rip the planet apart along with their invading enemies. Those Novians who escaped Babylon were tasked with beginning a new chapter in Novian history with those secrets safely in their possession. On board the Horizon Tory's guards secured Sigma, Zeal and their ship inside one of the Horizon lower hanger bays. Realizing their ship was now being approached by a large number of alien ships; they immediately opened a hyper-space portal and made the jump for home. Queen Dylan turned to her crew as the area around the Horizon ship turned bright blue and the ship disappeared. "Someone please tell me they know where that ship is headed!"

"Yes my queen, one of our vipers was able to land a tracker on the ship before it made its jump. Based on the coordinates they are headed to a small primitive galaxy called the Milky Way." Queen Dylan quickly gave out new orders, "broadcast the distress signal to all the other pernicious ships and transmit those coordinates to our people. That ship may be going to a land rich with food for us!" She stands up from her command chair, "Jaial be prepared to make the jump to those coordinates; but first I must do some house cleaning. Jada will you have our gunners target the hyper terminals on Arcia, Yolin and Jarmier nest simultaneously." The ship fell silent, Dylan turns to see her crew staring at her in astonishment. She shouted to the room, "treason will not be tolerated at all, and for their act the punishment will be to remain in this galaxy. I am not standing here asking for permission, I am giving orders. Jada is that possible!?" Jada cleared her throat to answer. "That will be difficult my queen, but we will make it work. But I must ask, what about their shields? Our missiles will never reach their targets!" Dylan gives Jada such a firm look that she took a step back. "Jada, the missiles you will fire have been programed to penetrate each of their shields, now don't waste time asking any more questions!" She snarled with her fangs showing as she spoke to Jada in a deep tone, "now get this done and don't miss!" Jada snaped to attention and yelled, "yes my Queen we will be ready on your command." Dylan returns to her chair while speaking, "now there is not an opening for this, so we must create one. Commander on my order, lower our shields and jam all surrounding signals. Then fire the hyper jets while cloaking the ship, giving the illusion that we have jumped back to our home world. While cloaked circle around behind those three rouge nests. Is that clear?"

"Yes my queen!" The tension on the command deck was already heightened from the current battle, but with this new mission the tension was now unbearable. The only sound coming from the deck was each person preparing to carry out the queen's orders. Dylan cleared her throat, "are we ready?" The command deck erupted with a "yes my queen!" Dylan smirked, "good then in 3, 2, 1 begin!" Arcia could see the hyper jet engines fire blue flames from Dylan's nest. She felt like their time was running out; "this may be the only opportunity to eliminate the high queen. If we damage her ship in the right place just before they make their jump the ship will disintegrate." She then decided to forgo their plan and shouted orders to her crew. "Open fire on the Alpha nest now while their shields are down! Target the vital areas of the nest!" Several missiles from the Eta nest headed for Dalen's. Yolin and Jarmier noticed Arcia's actions, and they both fell in line. Their nests joined in by opening fire on the Alpha nest. The three queens were only able to fire off a few missiles before the Alpha nest released large number of flares that detonated the incoming missiles.

The explosions emitted a bright light which concealed the Alpha nest. The three were unable to confirm if any of their missiles reached their targets. For fear of retaliation from the smaller colonies the three began to carry out their plan of escape. They each ordered their commanders to raise their shields and begin preparing to jump away from Novalucent. Arcia, Yolin and Jarmier spoke with one another over a secured signal. Arcia shouted, "can either of you confirm what just happened." Yolin and Jarmier answered simultaneously. "No!"

"Damn it, we had to do damage to her ship before they jumped." Arcia screamed at her crew, "someone find out if the nest disintegrated on its jump now!" Suddenly, it was apparent that Dylan was a few moves ahead of the three queens. All three of their commanders reported simultaneously that Dylan's nest was now targeting them. The queens screamed for evasive maneuvers, but it was too late. The Alpha nest fired three ARY missiles that traveled through each of the targeted nests shields and slammed into their hyper drive systems destroying them. Dylan's nest then made the jump for the Milky Way galaxy, minutes before Babylon fired its warhead. The war head was encased in metallic glass diamond shape casing, which cut through the crust and metal of the planet like wet tissue. Once it broke through the last layer of the planet, the casing was jettisoned so the warhead could directly contact the fiery planets core. The heat exploded the warhead on impact igniting the antimatter which created a reaction unlike any other. The ground above began to violently shake, as infrastructure all over the planet crumbled to the ground. Instantaneously the ground split open as a bright light escaped. That bright light was the last thing those ships around the planet ever saw, because following that light was the planet exploding. Sending out shockwaves and rubble that traveled millions of miles destroying anything it encountered. Most of the Pernicious nest were victims to the blast. The lesser colonies were so taken with what was going on between their high queen and Arcia, Yolin, and Jarmier that none of them managed to make the jump before the planet exploded. The ships that escaped the devastation were the Horizon, Dylan's nest and Azieal's nest. Azieal's nest was not able to make it to the Milky Way Galaxy because it was damaged by the shockwaves from the planet's explosion. They were forced to drop out of hyperspace millions of miles away from Earth. With sirens blaring on Azieal's nest, it was a welcome site for Dylan's three-dimensional image to appear on her personal communicator. Dylan smiled, "I am glad to see that you made it in one-piece Azieal." She shook her head no, "Not quite my Queen, our nest was damaged by the Novians weapon." Dylan face showed concern. "How bad is the damage?" Azieal looked around as the alarms and blinking lights ceased, "we have engine damage but still in one piece. Unfortunately, we will not be able to continue our journey to this new world you found." Dylan frowned at those words, "where are you now?"

"I am not sure, we lost navigation along with some other systems. I believe we are somewhere in the Gazomen galaxy. My queen this day has exacted a huge toil on our people; I do not believe many of our sister nest escaped that Novian weapon." Dylan flashed her fangs in disgust, "Aziel trust me we will rebuild our clan. This galaxy has a planet called Earth that is ripe with food for our people. We will secure the planet; you repair your nest and make your way here."

"Yes my Queen, it will take some time to repair, but we will be there as soon as we are able." Dylan wrinkled her nose in frustration, "Azieal I hear concern in your voice, what are you not saying to me?" There was a moment of silence before Azieal answered, with her voice trembling she spoke. "My queen we may be the last two Pernicious hives remaining..." Suddenly a flash of bright light appeared behind her followed by a loud boom. Azieal's image began to break up before disappearing. Dylan looks around the command deck to see surprised and concerned faces. She screamed, "get her back now, find out what happened and get her back!" Dylan could feel a sense of panic coming over her. They were embarking on never-before-seen territory without most of the advantages that made them the Pernicious. This moment of despair was being amplified by the fact that all eyes were on her. The Queen was leaning on the back of her command chair with her head hanging down. Sadu, her daughter, grasped the significance of the situation. She gracefully walked up the two steps to her chair and whispered into her ear. "My dearest mother, regardless of what happens next we must remain vigilant. It is the Pernicious way!" Those words were like fire in her bones, it was an immediate reminder of their legacy and her Pernicious lineage. She quickly straightened up, smiled at her daughter, then opened a channel so the entire nest could hear. "Attention! This is your queen; I know some of you may have concerns about our current situation. I am here to reassure you it will be fine because you're all aware of who we are, and what we're capable of! So, in the glorious name of the Pernicious let's go and conquer this new land for our people! We will rebuild our clan here and we will not stop until every single galaxy is conquered by the Pernicious!" Cheers erupted all over the nest, followed by the soldiers shouting the Pernicious war cry while beating on any and every surface available. Dylan turns and faces her Guardians with the look of pure anger. "Sci, prepare a scout team to go ahead of our nest; I want vital points of attack and a way to cripple this Earth planet quickly! Our campaign is not over!" The war cry on the command deck became deafening. The people of Earth had no clue that what is known as normal everyday life will soon never be the same.

CHAPTER 04

THE DISCOVERY

At 0430 AM the Horizon dropped out of hyperspace about 30,000 miles above Earth. The sensors at the Chronos headquarters lit up like fireworks on the fourth of July. The phone rings in Major Anderson's room upstairs. The Major sits up and takes a glance at his alarm clock to see the time before answering the phone. "Private you better have a good reason for waking me this early."

"Sir I do, we are detecting that the Horizons back and is now orbiting Earth." The Major jumped up from his bed. "Have you been able to make contact with anyone aboard?"

"No sir we have just been tracking the ship. Should I hail her?" The Major was clearly scrambling to get dressed. "No just stay locked on to her location; I will contact the brass and be there shortly." At 0610 AM the Major entered the nest walking at a brisk pace, the mundane sound of the room was interrupted by his booming voice. "Look alive men, we will be on with the President and joint chiefs in one hour. I need video conference up and running yesterday, and everything you have learned about the Horizon. I want to be able to answer any and every question about her when asked." The room exploded with motion! The personnel that were once dragging around the room doing their jobs, were now moving at light speed. The Major looked up from the table where he was sitting to see Sergeant Willow walking slowly in his direction. "Sergeant, I did not know that you were here.

"Yes sir I have been here since 5 this morning." Sergeant Willow now standing directly in front of the table, laid a blue encased tablet in front of the Major. "Sir, everything we've been able to gather on the Horizon ship since our sensors picked her up is on this tablet." The Major looked down and began to swipe through each page slowly, as if he was reading every word twice. He stopped on page 5 and looked up at Willows, "are we sure about this?" He said pointing at the tablet. "We are pretty certain sir; but we won't really know exactly what until we get on that ship!" The Major let out a deep sigh. "Knowing Tory, the way I do it won't be that simple. He has something up his sleeve; he will never just turn himself in." Willows, was surprised at that statement, "sir, do you think he will attack us with what he has on board the ship?" Anderson sat back in his chair, "I Can't say no for sure; he was really upset about his family being in Government custody, as well as the criminal charges brought against him. My money is on him trying to clear his name for his family's sake."

Willows gave the major a puzzled look, "but sir, why would we give him a chance to do anything. Since he's this close, we can just send a team of marines up there to take back our ship?" Anderson snaped back a quick response, "Negative sergeant, too much money went into building that ship. We need to protect that investment. I can't risk our men getting into a fire fight onboard and damaging the ship. So, we will just see what he has up his sleeve. If that doesn't go well; then we will show him the end of our gun barrels!" At that moment, a private enters the room, "sir, we are ready to connect with the President and Joint Chiefs." The Major gave a surprised look to the private, then grunts as he stands up from his chair, "that was quick!" The private still standing at attention knew that was sarcasm, quick was his expectation. Major Anderson looked directly at Willow, "well let's get this ball rolling."

Anderson, Willow and a private enter the conference room three floors above the Chronos nest center. Two soldiers were still placing binders of information about Horizon on the table. The Major and Sergeant both looked through the binders in front of them until they heard one of the privates make the announcement. "Sirs we are on with the President!" The large video screen came to life with the image of President Taylor sitting at the head of a large oval table with the Joint Chiefs. The soldiers in the room with Anderson snapped to attention. President Taylor salutes and says, "at ease men." Anderson got the ball rolling, "Good morning Mr. President."

"Good morning Major Anderson, so the Horizon is now back in our solar system?" Anderson flashed a weak smile, as he and Willows both answered, "Yes sir!" President Taylor leaned back in his chair, "so, gentlemen what can you tell us about the ship?" Major Anderson slid to the front of his seat. He looked as if he was still at attention while sitting down, "well sir our scans indicate the ship is intact; and from what we can detect the crew Tory used to hijack the ship are alive and well."

"Has there been any communication from Tory?" The President blurted out stopping the Major in mid thought. "No sir we have not heard anything from him, but I am sure he is aware that we know he is back." The president nods in agreement, "so, Major are there any indications of danger if we launch an offensive against him." Anderson paused before answering, attempting to choose his words carefully.

"Not that we can detect sir, but there is something you all need to be made aware of." That caught the attention of everyone in the room with President Taylor. "What is that major!?" The President asked with a confused tone. Anderson took a deep breath and began saying something that he didn't fully believe himself. "Sir, our sensors have picked up the presence of two beings on the ship that we believe are not human. We also have detected what we believe to be an alien craft stored in the lower cargo bay of the ship." The video screen showed a room full of confused men and women looking at one another. The room broke into chatter. President Taylor leaned forward in his chair and tapped on the table to silence the room. He was staring directly into the camera as he spoke with a look of disbelief.

"Wait, Major are you telling us that there are aliens and an alien craft on the Horizon?" Major Anderson cleared his throat, "yes sir, mister President, that is exactly what I am saying." The President had to again settle the room down because several conversations erupted after that statement. "So, does Tory or his crew know that they are on board?" Sargent Willow quickly interjected a response, "Mr. President, from what we can tell, he must know." The President leaned back in his chair now with a very serious look on his face. "How can you be so certain of that?" Sergeant Willows pressed a button on the remote he was holding and pictures from inside the Horizon control room appeared on screen for the President and joint chiefs to see. Willows took a quick glance at the major, and then began to explain the photos. "Mr. President the two figures you see here that appear to have a red tint around them are not human. That is the way our system displays objects when it does not recognize their molecular structure. From this prospective, it appears that Tory and his men are conversing with the two aliens." The President responded quickly to that statement. "How are you two so certain that these so-called aliens aren't holding Tory and his crew hostage?" Willow again glanced at the Major for permission to speak before answering. "Well, Mr. President that was a possibility we considered, but later deemed it unlikely because the members of Tory's crew, come and go as they wish. The two beings are the ones who seem to be confined, unable to move around the ship." There was a moment of awkward silence, the entire room was clearly digesting what they just heard. Someone outside the frame of the video was speaking in a low tone that was not being picked up by the microphones in the room. It was obvious to Anderson and Willow that whoever was speaking had the rooms undivided attention. Suddenly the President turned his attention back to the camera, "okay men, do you have any suggestions on how we proceed?" Anderson cleared his throat while looking at Willow, and Willow gave the universal head nod jester, that said you take that question. Anderson slowly looked back at the camera to respond. "Well sir, since we couldn't gain any intelligence on what Tory is planning. We suggest contacting him to get a dialogue going. Get him to make a mistake that will give us an angle of attack." The President rose from his seat hearing that, but before he could speak one of the joint chiefs blurted out. "Talk him down! He is an enemy of the state!" The President walked around the table and was now standing directly in front of the camera. "Gentlemen this man stole a ship worth 500 Billion dollars and disappeared for three years; that act made this country look like a laughingstock, and now you just want us to talk to this fugitive like he has done nothing wrong. Did you forget we don't negotiate with terrorist." Another one of the Joint Chiefs sitting outside of the camera's view shouted, "Mr. President now is the time for action, get our guys up there and take back that ship pronto, any other actions would be considered weak and unprepared!" "Mr. President." Major Anderson interrupts, "either way sir we still need time to gain as much intel on what our men would be facing if they must take the ship by force." The unseen voice chimed in again, "intel, we built the damn thing we should have all the information we need on what they will face!" The President walked back to his chair in deep thought, "you all make compelling arguments. General how long will it take to get a team ready to take back the Horizon?" The General smiled, "sir, we have four Talons on star port Vegas ready to dance. To get our teams up to speed, dressed and loaded into two of those Talons will take 45 to 50 minutes; another 30 minutes of travel time for the Talons to reach the Horizon. We could be storming the Horizon in less than two hours." President Taylor removed his glasses and began to clean them with the handkerchief from his jacket pocket. "Good, then General scramble your teams. Major put me in contact with Tory ASAP, because the clock just started ticking on when we take our ship back by force." The Major had to refrain from saluting with his response, "yes sir, Mr. President, we will be back in touch shortly!" President Taylor nodded to the camera in agreement, and the image on the screen went black. The Major exhaled, it felt like he had been holding his breath for hours. He stood up and addressed the room, "ok men, we have our orders, let's get this done quickly. Hail the Horizon!" One of the privates shouted, "sir yes sir!" A few unsuccessful minutes of being unable to contact Tory, evolved into a very tense situation. Major Anderson could feel the pressure of keeping the President and Joint Chiefs waiting, and he began taking it out on the room. His voice could be heard all over the nest floor, as he continued to shout out orders. Frustration was mounting in the room; it was becoming clear to everyone involved that no matter how much they wanted to make contact; without Tory responding their efforts were fruitless. Sargent Willow could not take his eyes off Major Anderson, just waiting for the blow up. He could see his clenched jaw from across the room. Everyone knew the President would not wait much longer, if they can't make contact, then he would replace them with someone who could. Suddenly, they hear a voice, and the black screen began to display a dark blurry image. "Major Anderson, long time no see, looks like you are sweating bullets." Tory said with a chuckle. The dim lit room, lit up as the large screen came to life with Tory's image. He was in a brightly lit padded light grey room somewhere on the Horizon. Major Anderson didn't breathe a sigh of relief; instead, he displayed anger with his response. "Tory what in the hell are you doing." Tory flashed a huge smile, the light glistened off his pearly white teeth. "Wait, please don't tell me they selected you to negotiate, they must not be aware of our past." Anderson shook his head no in response to those sarcastic remarks. "Tory let's just forget about our past for now; I am just here to help bring this situation to a peaceful resolution for all. You will be negotiating with the President shortly." Tory rolled his eyes and gave a very dry response, "then why am I still talking with you, where is the President?" Anderson threw up both hands in frustration, "Tory you are too damn stubborn, this situation has become quite toxic. Let me help you bring closure to this, what are your demands?" Tory leaned closer to his camera with a frown on his face. His voice had a sinister tone, "just shut up Major and do your job, I don't need a lecture. Get me on with the President, let's get this over with!". The Major sighs, then nods in agreement, "private connect us with the President and Joint Chiefs now." The private made a few keystrokes on a handheld device, then responded. "We are on with the President and Joint Chiefs sir." "Mr. President I have Tory on for you." President Taylor leaned back in his chair, "thank you Major, now Tory what will it take.." Tory shouted into his camera interrupting the President. "Mr. PRESIDENT! You and your flunkies are not in any position to speak. Understand this, I am the one in control here, I know that your military has begun prepping two Talons on station Vegas for lift off. If you want to try and use force to get back your precious ship then go ahead.

Just know you will not succeed and the lives of those young men and women will be on your hands; plus, you will never see your precious ship again. I am sure your sensors have already detected that I am returning with more than just this ship. You have one half hour to free my family and provide me with a full pardon for all the crimes fabricated against me." The President took a few moments to digest Tory's rant. He began to speak in a clear authoritative voice, "Tory, no matter what you have you will never be in a position to negotiate with us. Did it slip your mind that this country does not negotiate with terrorist." Tory sneered into his camera showing his bright white teeth again. "Today is the day that all changes because this so-called terrorist has acquired a special cargo that can be classified as a futuristic weapon. A weapon I am sure your enemies will be very interested in!" He paused his speech for dramatic effect, "Ahh yeah look at your joint chiefs faces; the language they all love weapons of mass destruction!" Tory stood up and grabbed his camera. His video feed moved erratically showing the floor celling, then finally his face. The feed shook as Tory screamed "I will give you a few hours to discuss and I expect a decision when I contact you!" The screen went blank. President Taylor looked around the room before responding. "Major Anderson, are there any indications that there may be a weapon aboard the Horizon?" Anderson now ringing his hands, clearly agitated by the current events, "sir we have run systematic scans on the Horizon several times and cannot detect any weaponry other than what was installed. However, the alien craft that is aboard the Horizon, has some type of shield around it that our sensors cannot penetrate. The weapon Tory is speaking about could very well be located inside the alien ship." Anderson could see a group of the Joint Chiefs huddled up behind the President having an intense conversation. He could hear the sounds of their voices but was unable to decipher what they were saying. His attention was snaped back to reality by the President's. "Anderson, find a way around that shield ASAP! We need to know exactly what is inside." The President paused as one of the joint chief's leaned over and whispers in his ear. He again looked directly into the camera, "Major, alert us if anything changes, we will be back in touch with you shortly!" The screen went black before Anderson could get out "Yes sir!"

Inside the White House the President and Joint Chiefs discuss the current dilemma facing them with the Horizon. The chairman of staff began the discussion, "Mr. President I believe that Tory is now more valuable to us than ever before. Not only is he a brilliant scientist but he probably possesses the knowledge needed to put this alien weapon to use!" The room erupts with voices of agreement from most of the Joint Chiefs. President Taylor showed some signs of irritation when he slightly raised his voice to the room. "First of all, we don't have any evidence of an alien weapon, not one shred! This could be a complete hoax." The chairman interrupted the President, "sir, I believe it would be too much of a risk for him to make this play without anything to bargain with. He has something up there that is very valuable; he would not show up like this unless he had something to leverage us with, this is freaking Tory Drew! Sir, I urge you to seize this opportunity!" The president took a closed stance with both arms folded across his chest. "How do we do that Mr. Chairman? How do we seize this opportunity?" The chairman smiled, "it's simple sir, we appease him by releasing his family but keeping them under close surveillance and agree not to file charges against him." The chairman paused his answer for dramatic effect. "That is if he agrees to work with our people to develop this alien weaponry." President Taylor looked around the room to see everyone with the look of agreement on their faces. "Gentlemen, I do not feel good about that proposal." The Chief Naval officer stood up and began walking around the table. "Mr. President, like the chairman said we must take advantage of this moment. Just hear me out; he only has a handful of the soldiers left over from his Prototype program on board the Horizon with him. Our military can easily overpower his people if we need to take the ship back by force. If we grant his request, and he agrees with our requirements; then we will have one of the most gifted minds of this century working for us for the rest of his natural born life." President Taylor gives an open mouth surprised look at the chief. "Did you say for life?"

"Remember sir we do not give into the demands of terrorist; he will have to answer for his actions. The US military will benefit greatly from his punishment." The President stands still staring at the entire group, hoping to see a face that objected to what was just proposed. He could not find one. "Does anyone here object to violating this man's civil rights for the remainder of his life?" The silence was deafening. The Secretary of Defense chimed in, "sir with all due respect we are dealing with unprecedented circumstances.

Tory forfeited his civil rights with his actions. Our actions must always be for the safety and wellbeing of this country." Taylor turns to face the blank screen on the wall. He stood there in deep thought for at least 5 minutes, no one in the room made a sound. He ran both hands through his hair while letting out a deep sigh. "If we do this, do we have a place to house Tory and his men?" The Naval officer quickly responded. "Sir, we have a rig in the Gulf of Mexico that will be perfect for this." The Army's Chief of Staff interrupted; "didn't the Navy already loose the Horizon ship to Tory and his men. Now you want the responsibility of keeping him and his cargo safe. I think not! Mr. President we have a black site that is heavily fortified in Virginia; that would be perfect."

"The Navy has not lost anything the Marines are responsible for security on Vegas."

The Marines officer quickly yelled out a response to that statement. "The Marines cannot secure anything when Naval officers are circumventing their every move. This loss is on you and your branch, just own that!"

"I will not own..." President Taylor slams his hands on the table to get the attention of the room. "Gentlemen this is on all of us! It is clearly obvious Tory had inside assistance to accomplish this crime." President Taylor turns to face Secretary of Defense Jaffer; "Jaffer, I do not want anyone to know what happens to Tory. Just keep me informed on what he reveals. This bad show you all want to put on is now your responsibility! Any blowback from this will land on your doorstep." President Taylor nods his head to the men and women in the room then turns and exits with his security detail. Once the door closed behind the President, Jaffer took over the meeting.

"Okay, we do not have a lot of time to get this organized. Be assured, we will have several opportunities to shift blame during the official inquiry, Until that happens, let's get our ship back. We will store the contents from the Horizon at the black site in Virginia. Tory and his people will also be thoroughly debriefed there. Once we have a clear understanding of what we're dealing with. Then we will have the rig in the Gulf equipped to handle the work we will need from our new discovery. Which will be the home for Tory and his men for the foreseeable future." Jaffer looked around the room to make certain everyone was still on board. "Gentlemen make that happen now!" The Naval and Army Officers shot to their feet, and both exited the room making calls on their cell phones. Jaffer continued to speak to the people remaining, "we will let him see and speak with his family during these negotiations, so I need them onsite ASAP! Afterwards we will house his family at our Millington Tennessee base." "We will also grant him a reduction in charges if he turns over our ship and its cargo and remains on as a lead scientist. Have our Talons establish a perimeter around the ship and be ready to breach on my notice!" Several conversations erupted in the conference room as the leaders began shouting orders to their people. Jaffer turned to one of the privates in the room, "private connect me with Major Anderson." The private made a few keystrokes on his tablet, and the black screen at the front of the room came back to life with the words searching for signal. Major Anderson appeared on the screen. He was surprised to see the Secretary of Defense standing in front of the oval table with an almost empty room behind him. "Jaffer, where is everyone?" Jaffer ignored that question. "Major, any word from Tory?" The Major was confused with the current situation and offered a halfhearted response, "no sir, he has not reached out to us and will not take our calls since he made his demands." Jaffer shook his head, "well has your group been able to determine what is in the alien craft?" Anderson took a deep breath and responded with an irritated tone. "No, we don't have any equipment that can get pass their technology. Whatever they have shielding the craft will not allow our equipment to get any type of visual." Jaffer sat in deep thought for a few moments before responding, "okay since he won't answer our calls and we aren't waiting for his deadline. Let's make him call us!"

Jaffer turns away from the camera to speak to the soldiers standing behind him, "relay my orders to have the Talons initiate docking maneuvers with the Horizon!" Anderson sat up in his chair completely astound at that order. "Jaffer are you sure about that order? Where is President Taylor!?" That snaped Jaffer's attention back to the camera, "well Major the President has been pulled away on another project. I will be running this program, and yes Major I'm sure about my order. Just be ready to connect me with Tory when he contacts you.

Moments later the two large black Talon ships packed with marines armed to the teeth began firing their thrusters, getting closer to the Horizon. Shortly after the Talons maneuvers, the video conference screen suddenly came to life for everyone with a visibly upset Tory. "Jaffer why the hell are you here? Where's the President?" Jaffer paused for a moment before responding. He flashed a tight smile, "Tory, I am overseeing these negotiations now!" Tory exhaled deeply throwing his head back in disgust. "Well now it all makes sense, I see your first decision is to attack. Still trying to start your own little war. Just know we will defend ourselves; this fight is your doing!" Jaffer shook his head from side to side to indicate no, "Tory, we all know that you placed yourself in this position, and the current events are a result of your actions so let's stop shifting blame. Accept some responsibility for your actions. We wanted to negotiate with you, but you issued demands, leaving us with no other choice." Tory grunted, "what, how can I negotiate when you have your marines locked and loaded headed in my direction?" Jaffer tight smile grew, in anticipation of his response. "Those ships are under my direct order, so what happens in the next 20 minutes will decide if I order them to attack or provide peaceful support. It all depends on what you do." Jaffer retrieved a tablet that was behind him, "Tory you can either surrender and allow one of those Talons to dock with the Horizon; and let our men take over. You will become the lead scientist on our future projects, your family will be moved back to Tennessee, and

I will sign orders reducing your charges keeping you out of prison for the rest of your life!" Tory hesitated before responding expecting Jaffer to say something else. "What if I don't agree..." Jaffer cut him off, "then your family who just arrived here, will get to see our Marines breach that ship and lay you and your men down! Come on Tory, those Talons are packed full of men who have not seen any combat in years and are itching for a fight." Jaffer leaned into the camera, his face consumed the entire screen, "Tory, you need to understand that the Horizon was just the first of its kind. We have more, and I have no problem with damaging you, the ship or its contents to regain control of it! I'm extending an olive branch to you, a chance to end this in a mannerable way. I'm transmitting a contract that outlines the stipulations I mentioned earlier. You have a choice, either sign it and end this peacefully; or don't and we remind you that you are a scientist not a soldier!" Tory sat frozen staring at the floor, he was not expecting the military to take such an aggressive approach. He looked into the camera; his bravado had faded away. For the first time Jaffer saw a chink in his armor. Tory blurted out, "where's my family? I want to see them!" Jaffer looks back at the door and motions to the security personnel. One of them walked out of the room and reentered with Tory's wife Kennedy. She was accompanied by two men in suits, one he recognized as their family lawyer. Kennedy froze when she saw Tory's face. She just stood there motionless with a look of astonishment; her eyes welled up with tears. Tory could tell she got dressed in a hurry. Her sandy brown dreads were pulled back into a makeshift ponytail. She didn't have on any makeup, but her honey brown skin still looked flawless. She was a welcome site for him, he didn't realize how long he had been away until now. "Kennedy?!! It is so good to see you!" Tory said while touching her face on his screen. In a frantic voice Kennedy responded, "oh my God Tory we thought you were dead! What the hell is going on, what are you doing?!" Tory took a deep breath, "I am securing our family's freedom forever!" Kennedy shook her head no while tears rolled down her face, "Tory all of this is crazy!

Stop this! Baby, please come home now your daughters need you, I need you!" Tory could hear his daughters in the background, "don't cry mommy, we told you we would find daddy!" Tory was not expecting negotiations to go like this. He was feeling an unexpected flood of emotions. He tried to push them down, "K you don't know these people like I do, they say one thing and do another." Kennedy broke down sobbing with her face in both hands. Seeing that sent shivers down his spine. Richard their attorney stepped forward. "Tory, I have reviewed this contract and it will keep you out of prison, you really don't have any other options. That is unless you want to risk never seeing your family again." Tory turned his back to the monitor talking with his men on board; the men gave a look of agreement with what he was saying. He turned back to the screen. He sat there for several minutes, with a closed fist in front of his mouth. His dark brown eyes peered into the screen, as Jaffer handed Kennedy tissues, and she began to compose herself. Tory spoke in a defeated tone, "okay Jaffer, we will stand down, go ahead, and send your people. I'm transmitting the docking codes to you now. We will go and prepare to receive them." Tory could see a smile form on his wife's face, a bright spot for him after what just occurred. Suddenly Secretary Jaffer appeared in front of her. "Excellent Tory you have made the right choice. We will be sending one Talon ship to dock and secure the Horizon. Shortly after that a freighter will be here to empty the contents. You and your men will be transported on the Talon to station Vegas along with the Horizon. Please understand that these marines have a fire first policy. You pull any tricks here this will end with a very different narrative." Tory, still staring at his wife's face on the screen mumbled, "I just want to see my family, no tricks." Forty minutes after the video conference the Talon ship docks with the Horizon. One of the docking bay doors slowly opens to reveal a team of five marines with their AR970 rifles ready to fire. Their green laser sites crossed one another creating a small light show inside the landing bay as they panned around the room. They exited the Talon in teams of five, until there were at least forty marines standing in the bay with their guns at the ready.

Their leader a six-foot-tall broad shoulder man, with an extremely muscular physique stepped forward. His military cut hair was fiery red and he shouted orders with a raspy voice, "breach the air lock now!" Tory had been standing right outside that door watching on the security cameras; before they could reach the door's control panel he punched in the code opening the door. At least ten of those green dots went directly to his chest with three or four more moving around his head. He slowly raised his arms. "Don't fire we surrender." The commanding officer walked through the doors followed by his men who never lost aim on Tory and the people standing with him. The leader of the marines chirped at Tory, "how many are on board?" Tory responded with a nervous voice, "we have about 10 men who are now running the ship and the four of us here."

"So that's it 14 of you?" Tory gave the marine an odd look, "well, kind of, we have 15 dead and 15 in stasis below." The marine gave a confused look back, "why are the men in stasis? Are they suffering from some type of alien virus?"

"No viruses, they are suffering from the effects of our genetics program, the stasis chambers are the only things keeping them alive." The marine nodded in acknowledgment of that information. "Okay, order your people to put the ship on auto pilot and report down here immediately." The marine then turned to his men and shouted out orders. "Split into your teams and sweep the entire ship, we meet back here in 30. If anyone or anything does not cooperate with your commands, kill it and we will sort it out later."

"Yes sir!" The marines shouted as they broke off into groups of five with very little conversation. The leader turned his attention back to Tory, "you, your men and the alien stowaways will board the Talon we came in with part of my squad." Tory stopped walking and looked back at the marine and asked, "why am I going to a space station and not

Earth where my family is?" The marine gave Tory a look of disgust for asking questions. He grunted, "all of you will be deprogrammed on station Vegas; once you finish your session then you will return to Earth." At that very moment the largest bay doors across the room from them opened. Revealing the inside of the freighter that just docked with the Horizon. Two more marines accompanying a heavy-set Lieutenant stepped into the cargo bay. The Lieutenant had a clammy white skin tone, his bald head and grey and brown mustache accentuated the permanent scowl on his face. He was an average-built man that had not seen a gym in several months. He immediately began shouting out orders. "Pack up everything that's not strapped down and get it on this damn freighter double time." He turned his attention to Sigma who was now standing behind Tory, with five guns still trained on him. Pointing at the alien craft he asked, "Is this yours?" "No, wait!" He shouted with both hands in the air as he turned to Tory while nodding his head towards Sigma. "Can this being understand me?" Sigma interrupted Tory's answer. "Yes I can understand you and yes that is my ship." The lieutenant flashed a surprised smile that quickly turned back to his normal scowl, "so, it speaks English!" He said with a sarcastic tone to Tory. He then turned back to Sigma, and said through clinched teeth, "then open it now please!" Sigma hesitated. The lieutenant raised his voice, "I will not ask again!" Sigma could feel the barrel from one of the rifles jammed into his back. He slowly walked over to the ship and ran his hand across a panel and the hatch opened. The lieutenant nodded, "good, men do it now!" Just then Sigma and Zeal both felt a sting on the back of their necks. They were injected with a tranquilizing agent that knocked them both out. Once those two bodies hit the deck, the lieutenant began barking out orders again. "Quickly get these two inside the containment chambers; we don't know how long those tranqs will last on them. Sweep this ship and empty the contents into the storage chambers on the freighter. Now Tory, I will need to see those men in stasis." Tory gives a confused look, "how do you know about the stasis chambers?" The Lieutenant pointed to his earpiece, "I've been listening to you the whole time. Now the clock is ticking, let's go!" Tory led the way to the ship's lab. The lieutenant was surprised to see the condition of the soldiers, "What the hell is wrong with them?" Tory turned away from the men like the answer was painful to give. "The same thing that has always been wrong with them, the genetic upgrades they were giving are now destroying their organs. These stasis machines slowdown their deterioration keeping them alive until I can figure out a way to save them." The lieutenant gave a confused look to Tory, "Can you really save them, they all look to be in pretty bad shape?" Tory was now peering into one of the stasis chambers, the look of graved concern covered his face. The lieutenant's question surprised him, "well, I really believe I can with the new nanotechnology that was introduced to me by my special friends; you know the two that you just knocked out." The lieutenant turned his back to Tory and taps on his com link, "patch me through to the Colonel." While awaiting a response, he began to walk around the room filming everything in sight with a handheld 3D camera. A deep voice interrupted the silence on the comm link, "Colonel Flack here lieutenant."

"Sir I am transmitting pictures to you now, of dying soldiers from Tory's old Prototype Project he believes he can save with new technology from these aliens." The line went silent for several minutes. "Sir? Sir do you read me?"

"A change of plans lieutenant for those stasis chambers, Tory and the aliens. All will be transported to our black site; I am transmitting the orders to you now!" "Sir Yes sir!" He then taps his com link twice to change the channel, "get me some personnel and equipment down here in the lab to move 15 stasis chambers!" He turned to his marine escorts who never let him out of their sight, "cuff him it is time for us to go." Both the Talon and freighter ships touch down at the marine black site in Virginia. Several men rush into the ship to place the two aliens in restraints. The lieutenant walked into the small bay where Tory was sitting.

He approached Tory with a set of restraints. "These are for you." Tory gives a look of exhaustion, "for me, why?" The lieutenant smirked, "we need to make sure you don't disappear again." Shaking his head, Tory stood up and faced the wall with both hands behind his back, "you really don't need those, this is your base, I have never been here, I'm not going anywhere." The lieutenant handed the restraint to one of the MP officers outside of the bay. He stepped out of the way while answering Tory, "this was never a request." The officer immediately rushed Tory to the floor as another officer entered to assist. They roughly put the restraints on him. Then the Lieutenant helped him to his feet while brushing the dust from his clothes. Tory staggered getting to his feet with both of his hands restrained behind his back, "what the hell lieutenant, that was completely uncalled for." The lieutenant laughed. "no sir what was uncalled for was the theft of a multibillion-dollar government craft. That was just a little reminder that you are not on vacation here. Now move!" They all exited the ship behind the two containment chambers that held the aliens to a waiting party which included Colonel Flack at the entrance of a hidden hanger door on the compound. Flack was 6-foot 2 slim white man, with snow white hair neatly styled in a military cut. The wrinkles on his face showed wisdom instead of age. He had a long scar that went from his right ear to below his mouth. His scraggly voice sounded like it was raised on a diet of expensive whiskey and cigars. He cleared his throat, "take those two chambers with the aliens to level D and keep them separated. This one here" he said, pointing at Tory, "goes with me. I will handle his debriefing myself." The MP's led Tory to what looked like a large freight elevator. The doors closed and Tory noticed there were only three floors to select. Flack placed his palm on the panel above the floor buttons. The scan lit up only one button with a star on it. Flack pressed it. After almost 3 minutes of riding down Tory realized there were far more than 3 floors to this place, and he may never see the outside again. Finally, they exited the elevator on who knows what floor. The walls of this floor were lined with eight small fishbowl rooms four on either side. Sitting directly in the middle of the room was a larger fishbowl that had one table and two chairs inside of it. The more Tory looked around the more he realized what he was looking at. In the back of the room there were two sets of stairs that led up to what looked like a control center. A control center that controlled the rooms on the floor.

Tory realized that these were not rooms they were cells. They had Tory standing in front of the large cell located in the middle of the room. Looking at the cell, there were no seems to indicate where the door was. It looked like one solid sheet of glass made the walls and ceiling. "What is this there are no doors, since when did you guys start building cells out of glass. Oh, wait this is just for show right. You put this glass box in the middle of the room to show case your awesome white desk and chairs." Colonel Flack stepped up to the cell and a control panel appeared out of thin air. He placed his thumb on a fingerprint scanner as a blue light moved across it. He then punched in a seven-digit code and an opening appeared. No doors, nothing slid open. Tory was astound at what he just witnessed. Flack turned to him and said, "it is metallic glass, now have a seat." The guards pushed Tory into the cell from behind; then removed his restraints. They exited the cell and Flack waved his hand over the scanner, suddenly the opening disappeared. Tory could see everything around him, but he could not hear a single solitary sound outside of the cell. Colonel Flack sat down across from Tory. He leans back in his chair never losing eye contact. Tory breaks the silence, "so am I under arrest, I thought I was not being charged with a crime?" The Colonel smiles, "I am obligated to tell you that everything that happens in this room is recorded." Tory looked around the room for some indication of what was happening, "okay Colonel, am I under arrest? If so I need my lawyer here now." Flack's raspy voice cut through the air, "now Tory we are simply here having a conversation, nothing more." Tory shakes his head in disbelief, "then what about my family? Where are they?" Flack leans forward with both elbows on the table separating the two. The long scar was all Tory could focus on, from here he could clearly see that the scar was made with a jagged weapon. His voice again cut the air, "now Tory, you have been to God knows where with an awfully expensive piece of US equipment, and on top of that you return with items and beings that you did not have when you left." Colonel Flack leans further forward pressing his hands on to the table. "So, let's just try this, you start talking about who helped you acquire the Horizon and everything, and I mean everything that happened after that, and I will stop you when I get tired of listening." Tory looks around the containment cube to now see several members of military brass looking in on this conversation. "Wow you bums aren't even hiding behind tinted glass anymore." Flack gives him a blank look before responding, "the seriousness of this situation eliminates the need for secrecy Tory." Tory smirked at the people outside of the cube, "well since this situation is so serious I believe I need my lawyer present." Flack smiled, "let's not act like you don't know what is happening now. Either you talk to the satisfaction of certain people here and you get to see your family or." He sat back in his chair folding his arms over his chest. Tory gives a puzzled look, waiting for him to finish the statement. Flack's smile melted into a very sinister look. He raised his scraggly voice to say, "or you will disappear forever!" Tory thoughts hung on those words and the quietness that surrounding them. A quietness that was now bothering him, it was too quiet, he could hear his own heartbeat. Suddenly Flack slammed his right hand on the table startling Tory and the people outside of the cube. "NOW, START TALKING!" Tory's mind was racing with different thoughts; he understood what these people were capable of. He could easily disappear and never see the light of day again; what would happen to his wife and kids. Tory slowly stood up having trouble catching his breath. "Okay wait can we slow things down, this feels like I will never see sunlight again!" Flack leaned over to look behind Tory at the people outside of the containment chamber. It looked like he was getting instructions. He started talking as Tory turned to see what, or who he was looking at. Flack responded, "you have my assurance that you are only here for debriefing. Once we finish this you will be moving on to your new assignment." Tory let out a deep sigh, "I'm not sure what your people want to hear from me." Flack leaned forward again, "you just start from the beginning, and I will tell you when to stop." While Tory was in Virginia reliving the events that happened with the Horizon over the last few years. Across the country two WSE engineers were on the brink of an unprecedented discovery.

The World Space Exploration, or WSE, largest campus located in the Florida Keys. James was doing his best imitation of an athlete running through the campus to escape one of the normal Florida pop-up thunderstorms. He made his way into the auxiliary of building A. There he saw his good friend Paul hard at work, "Paul, what in the world are you in here working on? You are running around here like the Flash." James stood at the entrance of the large office that was packed with server banks, old mainframe data storage systems, computers, and 3D video transmission ports. Without stopping Paul responded, "hey James, I am just up too one of my old hobbies." Paul was a short stocky balding white man known for his dry humor, intelligence, and novel hobbies. James, his best friend was a 6"4" slender dark skinned black man who was often mistaken on the streets for an NBA player, but around these parts was well known for his charisma, intelligence, and eidetic memory. These men fingerprints were on the majority of the latest space exploration breakthroughs that have happened in this facility, including the Horizon. "Damn Paul, you and your ancient technology; what are you tinkering with now?" Paul stopped in the middle of the room looking over his black framed glasses that were hanging on the edge of his nose. "Do you remember the Lunar Reconnaissance orbiter?"

"What, you mean the 40-year-old satellite that was orbiting the moon? "

"Yeah James that is the definition of lunar orbiter!" Paul said snarky. James chuckled at his remark, "so, what the hell are you doing with it?" Paul was now standing in front of a main frame computer, typing at a ferocious pace. "I was able to get it back online and it started taking photos again." James gave a puzzled look to Paul, "wait, let me get this straight, we have successfully created a hyper drive system that allows us to travel to unknown solar systems in a matter of minutes, and you are concerned about photos of earth's moon? I mean literally down the hall they are downloading data gathered from whatever galaxy the Horizon traveled to; that doesn't interest you at all?" Paul looks away from the main frame with a sarcastic look on his face. "Yes It does but I think there is something in these photos! I just need to figure out what is showing up on the pictures." James shakes his head in disbelief, "my guess it's moon dust and rocks!" He let out a hearty laugh that echoed down the hall. Paul stopped moving and was now staring at James with the look of disapproval. "No, I mean it looks like something is affecting the lens. Like maybe something is on the Lunar satellite."

"What!?" James shouted. "Come on Paul the lens was probably cracked from some type of debris; this is a huge waste of your time, and now I regret that I asked what you were doing." Paul let out an irritated sigh, looking up to the ceiling, "well there has not been any data that would support the satellite being struck by debris; and most importantly tell me what this looks like?" Paul brings up images on one of the 3D projector screens in front of them that were captured by the Lunar orbiter. "I have been using the latest photo software to clear these images up, they were taken with an older camera." James lets out a sarcastic sigh, "that's true you can actually make out details in the photos. Detailed rocks and dust" Paul motioned his hand from right to left to change images. "Just keep watching James."

"Ok Paul, I see dirt", the image changed "more dirt", the image changed again "dirt with a large black spot? What is that something on the lens?" Paul jumps up from his seat waving his hands above his head, "finally you hear me, I thought that something happened to the lens; but look at the black area of the photo." Paul enlarged the photo, "it has stars in it." James was now sitting on the edge of his seat, completely engrossed in the photo. "Stars?!! How can the satellite be picking up pictures of space when it clearly has the moon directly in front of it?"

"Well James, I believe I have exhausted all possibilities, including the trajectory of the satellite orbit being off, or the lens is somehow moving. Then I saw this." Paul quickly went through 8 or 9 photos and stopped on one. "Ok wait, now this one is definitely a photo of space." James took control of the program; he was working to bring more clarity to the photos. "It's weird that a stationary camera is capturing space when facing the dark side of the moon. The stars in the photos even look distorted, like they are in clusters." Paul nodded his head in agreement, "yeah that does look like an odd group of stars." Paul now standing in front of James pointing at what James assumed was a cluster of stars. James then began to move both hands around the image, moving them outward to zoom in and clear the image. Once the image became clear Paul dropped his glasses on the table. "Paul, what is that!!!?" James asked with a mixture of excitement and confusion. Paul then shouted orders to the A.I. system. "SANS bring up a picture of the Lunar Reconnaissance orbiter!" The picture appeared next to the current photo they were looking at. "That James is the reflection of the orbiter." James turns and looks at Paul in disbelief, "what the hell is it reflecting off of?" Paul gave a grave look of concern, "that I don't know but I am certain we don't have anything on earth that can do this." Paul began to pace back and forth, "this is huge we need to call someone we can't sit on this!" James eyes were still glued on the photo, "Paul, do you think this can this be something from the Chinese?" Paul still pacing and mumbling to himself, "whoever this is, they decided to hide it on the dark side of the moon; that can't be good for any of us. We need to alert someone!" James finally takes his attention off the photo to see Paul working himself into a frenzy, "wait, calm down Paul let's just pause for a beat. I just want to be sure this is not an anomaly before we make a statement like that. So how long have you had this?" Paul stopped to think, "at least a week, it took a few days to get the photos scrubbed to really be able to see anything." James clapped his hands, "okay, the orbiter has cleared the dark side on its latest orbit. It should have transmitted some new pictures. Let's scrub those and see if we get the same thing." Paul had an unsettled look on his face, "James, are you crazy? What if that thing moved. This can be a serious threat! We need to inform someone ASAP." James, ignoring that statement, moved to the mainframe, and started typing on the keyboard. "Paul, you know we need more evidence than one photo to present to our executives. We don't know how long, whatever that is, has been there. I just fine-tuned the programing to scrub the photos faster. We should have something solid in a couple of hours to present." Paul reluctantly agreed. "Look at it this way Paul, this finding can give you a chance to check off an item on your bucket list. This will have you in a room presenting to the President." Paul just stared at James with a blank look, "I always dreamed of sharing groundbreaking technology with the President. Not the possible discovery of a national threat!" James chuckled at that statement. "Let's not get ahead of ourselves." Attempting to lighten the mood, James tried changing the subject. Pointing to the monitors hanging from the ceiling, "so, those monitors are dedicated to gathering data from the orbiter?" Paul slowly nodded his head, "yes, those four screens are related to the orbiter. Signal strength, location, data feed, basically anything the orbiter can transmit will be found on those screens." Just as Paul said that all four of the screens went blank. Paul shouted, "what the hell? What did you touch James?" James quickly stepped back away from the monitors with both hands in the air, "I didn't touch anything." The frustration with this moment was clearly obvious in Paul's actions and voice, "just move!" Paul started typing a few keystrokes, then began checking the mainframe connections. "Could it be solar flares interrupting the signal?" James asked with a confused tone. Paul looked up from the mainframe with a grave look of concern. "James, it's gone!" Paul said turning his attention to a single monitor behind them. James still confused and looking to make sure the power cords were plugged in completely, "what's gone?" Paul lets out a loud breath, "the orbiter! The orbiter is no longer there." James froze just staring at the black monitors, "are you sure this is not just some type of interruption in its signal?" Paul moving across the room, directs James's attention to a six-ty-inch monitor on the wall to the left of the main entrance. "This system is tracking the location of every US satellite, even if something like a flare interrupted the signal, we would still be able to see the expected trajectory here in grey. Once it reconnects with the orbiter's signal it corrects the trajectory and changes it to the green color you see for all the other satellites. When I type in the ID code for the orbiter it just shows the history of its path in red, this only happens when the system detects a significant event with the satellite being searched for." James gave Paul a graved look, "what type of event?" Paul dropped his head, "red in-dicates catastrophic." James shuddered at that statement. He then quickly moved to the back of the room, "let's hurry up and get the last batch of pictures ready to present; I de-finitely believe that it is time to contact somebody in the department of defense!" Paul quickly followed as he shou-ted, "oh now you want to contact someone!" James looked up from the monitor, "okay I admit that I was wrong, the current events have escalated my level of concern. Whoe-ver or whatever that is, now know that we have detected their hiding place." Paul froze, "so then, what's next? Inva-sion?!!" James let out a deep sigh, "not sure but we need those photos finished! While you do that I will start rea-ching out to our brass." James jumped on the phone trying his best to get through to someone in Washington. The pro-blem was that an engineer could not just pick up the phone and directly call the secretary of defense. He ended up on the phone with one of his superiors trying to explain what they had when Paul interrupted him. "James, just tell him we are bringing everything to him, because we now have video evidence." The two men scrambled gathering things and bolted out of the room.

A day later they both found themselves in Washington DC. Commander Wright, Paul, and James were following one of the Presidential aids walking through the halls of the Pentagon; headed to a meeting. They could hear the conversations from within the room ten feet from the door. The conversations sounded intense just based on the volume. As the three men entered the room, the conversations slowly died down. People were spread out all over the room, and on cue they started to take their seats. The aid turned to the men, "who will be speaking?" Paul and James responded simultaneously "I will." They both chuckled at that. Paul spoke up, "well we both will." The aid logged onto a tablet that turned on the 105-inch screen behind them, without speaking to either of the men he verified that their presentation was loaded on the tablet. He looked at the three men, "do either one of you know how to work this system?" Paul quickly responded, "yes I am familiar with it."

"Good, the President will be here soon he will let you know when to present your information, until then have a seat." Shortly after the aid placed the tablet on the table, a door to the right of the LCD screen opened. In stepped two secret service agents, followed by the chief of staff, the Vice president, and finally the President. Paul took a glance around the room, and everyone was standing at attention. He never imagined in his wildest dream that he would be here, in the same room as the President of the United States presenting him information. His grandkids, grandkids will be talking about this moment. He was snapped back to reality when the President began speaking. "At ease, let's get started." Everyone took their seats. The president and his chief of staff sat at the opposite end of the table from Paul and James. "So, gentlemen we do not have all day what is it that is so important?" The Secretary of Defense spoke up. "Mr. President, sir we have two WSE engineers here," he looked down at his notes in front of him, "Paul and James, these two men have made a significant discovery." The president dropped a pamphlet on the table, "this briefing says this discovery was made on the moon." The secretary hesitated, startled from the president's action. He cleared his throat, "that is correct Mr. President; they managed to reconnect with our lunar orbiter and got pictures of an object on the dark side of the moon." Just then the Air Force Admiral sat forward, "wait we had to have an emergency meeting for something on the face of the moon, anything significant would have been discovered by one of our military satellites." James leaned over to Commander Wright and Paul, "Commander, what all did you tell the Secretary?" The commander leaned in and whispered, "I told him everything the two of you told me." Paul could no longer take the direction of this discussion, he let out a deep sigh and stood up, "excuse me Mr. President may I?" he said gesturing towards the LCD screen behind him. A silence fell over the room. President Taylor responded to him "by all means, yes please enlighten us." Paul made a few keystrokes on the tablet and the photos they were working on appeared on the screen. "James and I were going over photos taken from the lunar satellite. The object in question is not on the face of the moon, it is one hundred miles from the surface and matching the moons orbit to remain on the dark side." The Secretary of defense blurted out, "are you certain about this?" Paul gave a firm smile, "yes Mr. Secretary we are pretty certain about this." Paul looked at James and James brought up a picture on the screen that again silenced the room. "Gentlemen you can see on this photo that whatever the satellite took a picture of has a reflective surface. We can clearly see the satellites reflection along with its flash in this photo. We know this object is not on the surface of the moon." After this image was captured, I changed the direction of the satellite's orbit to go within

200,000 miles of the moon's surface, and to make a recording using its ultraviolet lenses. James will you please play the video." The President sat up straight in his chair as the video played. "Is that what I think it is?" The video showed an image of what looked to be four huge, connected hornet nests made from mercury. "Well Mr. President," James responded, "you can clearly see that this is definitely some type of craft, we estimate it to be about twice the size of Texas." President Taylor quickly turns to the secretary of defense, "none of our systems detected this?" The secretary responded with concern in his voice, his eyes were still glued to the screen. "No sir, our systems should have detected a ship that size long before it got that close to the moon." The President motioned for his aid to come to him, while the video continued to play to a stunned audience. President Taylor had a million questions going through his mind. The problem was he had no answers for any of them, and he needed some fast. His aid reached him, "listen get copies of these photos and video to Colonel Flack. Have him check with Tory to see if he has seen any vessels like this during his journey." Paul looks at James with wide eyes; James whispers, "did Tory discover some extraterrestrial beings on his trip?" Paul felt a knot in his stomach as he whispered back, "or worst, did they follow him back to earth." James facial expression went blank. For the first time these two realized that this discovery could be detrimental to life on earth. President Taylor attention shifted back to Paul and James; "is this alien craft still there? Is the satellite still filming this?" Paul gave the president a grave look, "unfortunately, sir we lost the satellite's signal." Paul and James could hear mumbling around the room in response to that statement. The look of concern was starting to show on President Taylor's face. He gave them both a stern look with his response. "Wait gentlemen, expound on that for me do you mean you lost the satellite's signal or the satellite?" Paul hesitated to respond, as he looked around the room. All eyes were on them. He was now beginning to really feel nervous. It felt like a lump formed in his throat as he tried to speak. "Sir, we are not sure." The President responds in disbelief, "I don't need uncertainty now I need answers!" James realizing Paul was struggling with this situation blurted out a response. "Sir, we believe the satellite was either destroyed or captured. Whatever was done, it has stopped any transmission, we have not been able to detect it with any of the dedicated tracking equipment." President Taylor sat up in his chair and raised his voice in his response. "So, you're telling me that right now we cannot tell where that thing is," while pointing at the infamous object frozen on the screen. His voice raised a few more octaves, "you're saying that right now, we don't know whether it's still on the dark side of the moon or entering earth's air space! This situation has become very concerning. The fact that whoever or whatever this thing is, went out of the way to hide their presence in our atmosphere doesn't sound too peaceful to me." President Taylor gave Paul a death stare. Paul felt like his eyes were burning a hole into his forehead. He glanced around the room hoping that someone would get the president's attention. Finally, the presidents aid walked back into the room. President Taylor nodded for the aid to speak, "sir, Tory confirmed that this thing, is an alien ship. He encountered similar vessels on his journey with the Horizon." A low rumble of conversation began in the room. The President now staring at the image on the large HD screen. Takes a deep breath then shocks the room with his statement. "Gentlemen we are now at Defcon 1; someone have a team from the Eagle space station get out there and get a location on that damn ship!" "Mr. President," the Secretary of Defense Jaffer chimed in, "sir are we jumping the gun on setting the threat level that high? We really don't know if this is an actual threat." President Taylor gives Jaffer a look of anger, "that is true, we don't know if this is a threat right now. I don't know anything that makes an effort to conceal its presence like this peaceful." The President places both of his hands on the table and looks around the room. "I need everyone in this room to understand that we've just learned that humans are not alone in this world. Unfortunately, I never believed I would be saying this, but it is time for us to prepare for a full-scale invasion." The room erupted; and Jaffer quickly stood up. "Invasion! Mr. President that may be a stretch; this could easily just be the Chinese or Russians."

"Calm down people calm down!" President Taylor shouted to quiet the room. "Let me ask all of you does anyone in here, have any intel on countries building anything on this scale?" Silence fell over the room. "That's what I thought; you all heard that Tory confirmed this to be an alien craft. In his debriefing, he spoke about witnessing several of these types of ships making a full-scale invasion of a planet in the newly discovered galaxy. If someone can provide an explanation for an object that looks just like what Tory witnessed, remaining in the shadows of our moon to be anything other than aggressive. Then I will listen? Until then we will have to treat this as the serious threat that it is." Someone in the room shouts, "sir, can we at least wait to see what our team from the Eagle station reports back about the ships location; before making plans of defense and evacuation?" The President takes a long deep breath. "My concern is that right now these aliens know that we know they are here. When they detect one of our Talons then what? That may very well be the start of something we are not prepared for. I prefer that we are ready for whatever comes." Another question comes from around the table, "what is our next move? If they are a threat we can't wait for them to attack, we need to eliminate them now!" Taylor paused to deeply consider that, "I need a meeting with the world leaders, this is an Earth problem and will require a formulated response from all of us. No evacuations yet and no media! For now, this information does not leave this room!" President Taylor's aid chimes in, "sir we will not be able to keep this under wraps for long, the media will expect something when you take an emergency meeting with the world leaders." President Taylor paused for a moment considering how to answer that. "That is true, but I need everyone in this room to stall on any explanations for the media for as long as they can. My office will let you know when and what you can share with the media, and someone put these two on ice!" The President said pointing at Paul and James. "They do not leave until I say so. Now let's move people!" The room exploded with activity and communication. Paul and James sat in stunned silence. Then they both turn to Commander Wright; Paul asks so where do we go from here? The dismayed look on the Commanders face set off panic in both men.

CHAPTER 05

THE ALLIANCE

At 0800 hours, the members of the crew were preparing their gear for this mission. Houston would be in to brief them on the particulars, but they already knew this was a retrieval mission at a highly secured military base. Houston and Nicole walked through the conference room that led into one of their many weapons storage rooms on the compound. They were surprised to see the entire crew sitting around the room packed and ready to go. Houston blurts out, "wow the entire crew is ready to roll, I like that. Let's move this to the conference room." Khairi spoke up during the short walk, "so let me get this right we are going into this black site to retrieve some confiscated metal that came back aboard the Horizon?" Houston takes a seat at the head chair; he pulls out what looks like a flat keyboard stand. He connects a flash drive, and from the middle of the table pops up a three-dimensional map of the targeted military base. Houston looked at Khairi, "yes that is correct Khairi." Khairi lets out a long breath, "so what has that metal got to do with this group? Houston made a few keystrokes and a virtual image of the metal appeared above the table. Houston sat forward as he began to explain, "the metal that was aboard Horizon has some of the same components as the materials that was used in the Prototype program. Since you three are a byproduct of that program this metal may be far more beneficial to you than our U.S. Government." Kya quickly responded, "but Houston, you don't operate on assumptions, so this metal must have some real promise for us to break a few hundred laws by stealing it from a level five secured facility." Houston smiled, "well, the truth is Kya we need that material if we ever want to defeat these Pernicious aliens. Plus, a bonus for us is that the base will not be fully staffed. Our military is stretched thin trying to turn back this invasion." Houston stands up with a remote in his hand, "look this will be a very quick mission, we get in, get the goods and get out!" A blue laser from the remote illuminates an area on the three-dimensional map, that took the place of the metal image. "Okay listen up guys this thirty-five-story building is where the metal is being stored. The Scorpion will approach from the South end of the compound teleporting you guys down into the building. We will locate a safe zone to drop you in; you will have to attach teleport sensors to the metal, radio the ship and they will transport the team and metal out." Khairi leans back in his chair "let me guess, we have to locate the package ourselves right?" Houston smiles again, "you will have a sensor that Squirt designed that will lead you directly to the package, we believe it is somewhere on the 30th floor, piece of cake right! Oh, and one more thing there should be a skeleton crew working at the base so you should not run into any confrontation, but if you do remember we are on the same team they just don't know that.

On this mission you will be using non-lethal force if contacted! Dust off in 45 minutes." Everyone began to stand up from the table when Nicole blurts out, "oh, one more thing!" Reaching in her pocket she pulls out a flash drive and slides it across the table in the direction of the triplets; "we need for you guys to tap into their network and download any information they have that may be of value to us." Kimoni slowly stood up from the table, "you know every time you say we are running a simple in and out mission, it always turns into one of our most difficult operations. We are not just invading a US black site, now we've got to hack into a military network and download information!" Nicole smirked at the three of them, "no guys, with this flash drive all you'll need to do is connect it to their network, the drive will do all the heavy lifting. I would never send you guys out there naked!" Kimoni gritted his teeth, "I know Nicole just a little frustrated because our missions keep going from routine to extremely dangerous and we're getting nothing out of them. Feels like we are just valets for the government." Kimoni shot Houston a fiery look as he paused to hear the silence in the room. Then with a sarcastic tone said "Yeah, if that's all then let's go." Nicole whispers to Houston, "sir you may need to have a talk with Kimoni before he completely checks out." Houston just nods to Nicole and exits the room. Nicole grabs Kimoni's arm, "one more thing." She hands him a case with extra teleportation sensors in them. Kimoni gave a puzzled look, "what are these for?" Nicole gave him a slight smile, "just in case yall find something you just can't leave without." Kimoni, picks them up with a smile then stores them in his chest plate. The crew gathers their gear and exits the conference room.

U.S. Black Site, Virginia:

At 1030 hours that night, the Scorpion ship entered Virginia airspace, cloaked to avoid any detection. "CB we will reach the black site base in 15 minutes." CB voice comes in on the scorpions' intercom. "come in Khairi."

"Yeah CB go ahead."

"We will be ready to teleport in 15, we did a sweep of the building for life signs, there seems to be more activity in the building than we expected." Khairi shakes his head while looking at Kimoni, "CB we are ready." Kimoni spoke up, "like we have a choice in this!" CB froze for a second, not expecting that.

He ignored it and quickly jumped back on the mission objective. "Okay, squirt has located a safe place to teleport the team, it is located on the second floor; once inside you guys can locate the payload." Kimoni shouts, "the second floor, main this just gets better by the minute, what's next CB?'

"That's it guys, we get you in you do your magic and we will get you out." Squirt chimed in, "ok we have locked down the location and opening portal in 3,2,1 go fast and hard guys!" Khairi shouts "10-4 Squirt, Ambassadors let's roll" Khairi led the triplets through the portal. He could never get use to this type of travel; you enter a bright portal and exit the portal in God knows where. You must completely trust your crew that your exit point is clear of any danger. Passing through the portal was always the same, a blinding light, with no sound. The only sensation was the ice cold feeling he felt on every inch of his body. Like walking through an industrial cryochamber set on max. The best thing about this ordeal was their heads-up display on their helmets. It is always on and operating when they exit. Squirt spins in his co-pilot's chair to look back at CB, "the triplets are safely away CB."

"Good Squirt, take us up to 10,000 feet and go weapons hot just in case we have to shoot our way out of here." The three warriors exited the portal in a storage unit inside the compound; they are dressed in their black polymer lightweight body armor. The three of them all feel these suits are uncomfortable, but they also know how good the suits are. The suits can stop small caliber rounds, knives, and machetes. They are also equipped with cooling and heating units to mask their infrared signatures; as well as being designed to conceal all the weapons needed without slowing them down. Their helmets included earpieces that encrypted their communication and provided them with a voice activated display with thermal readings, infrared, motion detection and navigation. Khairi uses a small extension camera to check the hallway in both directions outside of the room they were in. "The hallway is clear, Kimoni have you located the package yet?"

"Yeah I have a lock on it; it is twenty-four floors directly above us."

Kya sighed while shaking her head, "Houston missed it by 4 floors, we have to navigate twenty-four floors up, that defiantly ends the so called simple in and out mission." Khairi grunted, "true! CB we have located the package on the 26th floor, we are moving now to secure. Be ready to bring us home!" "Great Khairi, we will be ready!" Khairi slowly and quietly opens the storeroom door.

"Let's move, Kya you lead the way." The three head down the corridor for a stairwell. Squirt quickly looks up from one of his control panels, "hey CB I thought there was supposed to be a skeleton crew at this site?" CB looked at him confused, "yeah Squirt that's what our Intel said, you got something different." Squirt gave a panicked look, "I have something very different," Squirt punched a few keys to bring the display up on the main screen. "I'm showing a lot of activity on the twenty sixth floor, I see at least 30 life signs moving around up there." CB slams his fist on the arm of his chair, "damn it, they're headed straight for an ambush!" Squirt opens a channel on the com link for CB. "Ambassadors come in." Kya responds, "go ahead CB." He took a deep breath, "listen, you are headed into a hot zone." Kya holds up her fist and her brothers stop behind her in the stairwell. She whispered, "where are the bogies located CB?" The anxiety of a failed mission gave CB severe dry mouth, he could barely get his words out. "We are reading at least 30 bogies on the 26th floor!" Kya grits her teeth, "great just freaking great, that is where we are headed." CB cleared his throat trying to find relief, "Kya, it looks like they are clustered in one room, you three may be able to retrieve the payload without confrontation, but you will have to be invisible." Kya lets out a chuckle, "go invisible, yeah that's something we can do." She looks back at her brothers and whispers in their com links, "you heard him, we have bogies between us and the payload. Let's keep it quick and clean and go home like we came here!" Khairi and Kimoni both responded with a simple head nod. The three continued their ascend until they reach the door to the twenty sixth floor hallway. Khairi inserts an optical wire under the hallway door. Kya breaks the silence; "I am transmitting the location of the payload to your nav screens." The right-hand corner of their face shield displayed the location of the payload, as well as the lay out of the 26th floor. They both respond simultaneously, "got it!" Khairi removes the fiber optic from under the door, "ok the hallway is clear, but the nav screen says we have two guards outside of our desired location. On the exit, Kya you watch our six until we get to the end of the hallway. Then you play distraction for the guards, and we will drop them; Kimoni you are high I am low. The neutralize guards will be secured inside the storage room. Once inside, Kimoni you plug into the network and download whatever Houston is looking for; Kya and I will prepare the payload." Kimoni and Kya both nod accepting the plan while cocking their handguns. Khairi cracks the door and checks for movement; there was none, he whispered, "okay let's move!" The three exited the door quickly and quietly; they were down the 70-foot corridor in no time. They stopped at the corner of the wall. Standing outside of the large doors on 26 West were two-armed MP soldiers who considered themselves ready for any situation, any situation other than what they were about to face. Out of nowhere a female appears from around the corner. The soldiers knew from the way she was dressed there could be trouble, but this was a woman, she was no match for the two large soldiers. She turned towards them smiled and began to slowly walk in their direction. The soldiers lost focus for one moment admiring her shapely figure as she walked toward them. That one moment of laps was all Khairi and Kimoni needed. They swung around the corner with guns drawn in both hands; the guards could not get out a word or get their M16's up to fire before there were two darts in both of their throats. The neurotoxin tranquilizers took immediate affect and the soldiers dropped to the floor like anchors. Kya quickly ran to the doors keypad and began to hack it with her tools. Kimoni and Khairi each pick up a soldier. Kimoni whispers while watching the other end of the hall for movement, "are you good Kya?" "Yeah just a couple of seconds – there got it!" Swoosh, the door opens, and they enter the room. As the door closed behind them; Khairi quickly changed his comm link signal with a double tap to his ear, "CB come in."

"Go ahead Khairi." Kahari voice indicated that he was moving around the room swiftly, "we have located the payload we will have it ready in five."

"Great we will begin preparations for our approach to pick you guys up." Kimoni immediately went to a network server and installed the jump drive Nicole gave him. It downloaded a program that broke through the firewalls and defenses, located the files Houston and Nicole were interested in and began copying them. While Nicole drive was working, Kimoni began to tour the room. He walked into what looked like a clean chamber to find two aliens restrained in two clear chambers that were built like coffins. He whispered into his comm link to his brother and sister, "hey you guys need to check this out. I believe I just found the aliens Houston told us about." Kya responded "really, I thought he said it was one?" Kimoni spun back around to be sure, "well, there are two in here now and they definitely don't look human." Kimoni took a long look at the larger alien. His skin was dark with a purple tone to it and looked like it was made from gravel. He was dressed in gold and white armor. "Are they dead?" Kya asked. Kimoni whispered, "not sure, they are restrained now, it looks like they may have been tortured." Just then Sigma's eyes opened startling Kimoni. He raised his voice speaking into the comm link, "they are definitely alive!" Kimoni removed his helmet so the alien could see his face, he whispered while using over exaggerated motions to pronounce his words. "Can you understand me?" Sigma gave a painful looking smile, then spoke English, which surprised Kimoni.

"Your eyes look familiar, are you of Novian descent?" Kimoni gave him a puzzled look, "Novian, what the hell is that?" Sigma took a deep breath clearly uncomfortable from what was done to him, "those are the people from my home world Novalucent." Kimoni quickly shook his head no, while putting his helmet back on, "no, I am a human from Earth." Sigma struggled to speak louder, "I see our ancestors in your eyes." Just then Kya's voice came in on Kimoni's headset startling him. "Are you still playing with those aliens?" He turned expecting to see Kya in the room with him, "hey I believe they overcooked one of these guys. He asked was I a Novian from Novalucent." Kahari chimed in, "Novalucent, didn't Houston say that is where the elements used in the Prototype Program came from." That froze Kimoni. "He responded while looking directly at Sigma, the Prototype Program mom and dad were in?"

"Exactly! Now let's get ready to roll out," Khairi responded. Kimoni could now see the unique gold tint to Sigma's eyes, a tint that was like his sibling's eyes. He asked him, "so you believe we are related?" Sigma shakes his head no; "it is deeper than that. You all are here for the metal right?" Kimoni quickly responded "Yes!" Sigma smiled; "the men here, that are preforming these tests on us will never see the true potential of anything that is in my ship, not like you!" Kimoni now intoxicated with interest as he crept closer to the alien, still amazed at how his skin looked, "what do you mean by that?"

"My young one, we do not have enough time you all will have company very soon." Kimoni could feel the adrenalin rushing through his veins as he remembered they were on a mission; he lost all focus talking with this alien. He turned in the direction of the room where his siblings were, while pulling the teleportation sensors out of his vest. "Hey guys, our payload just increased." Khairi froze hearing that, "what the hell do you mean increased Kimoni?" Kimoni casually responded, "we are taking the aliens!" He then opened a channel for CB. "Go for CB!"

"What's up Kimoni?"

"The payload is ready." Squirt blurts out "cool I have a lock on it and you guys."

"Not us, not yet Squirt. Nicole's program is still hacking their network, take the payload and give us a couple of minutes." Squirt replied "okay" with a puzzled tone, 'hey the payload is larger than I expected." Kimoni quickly responds "is that a problem. Squirt? Squirt!?" Squirt stammers, "no, not a problem Kimoni; all of it is now safely aboard the ship." All three of the Ambassadors let out a sigh of relief.

There was commotion among the military personnel stationed in the security nest on the first floor of the building, "Captain Rose come in!" The Captains deep voice responded on the comm, "go ahead private." "Sir someone has hacked into our network and is downloading files." Captain Rose was puzzled by what he just heard, he paused for a minute before answering, "private this facility is completely offline; no one should be able to get into our network!" The private responds with slight panic in his voice, "yes sir that is true, but whoever this is they are currently in the building, and they are downloading some large files." The panic began to spread through the room. Captain Rose yelled over the coms, "can you stop them, stop what they are downloading?!" The private was now joined by a few of his colleagues, they were all franticly typing on different keyboards and tablets. "No sir, we can't stop them, or lock them out!"

"Damn! Initiate a lockdown of the facility and get me their location! Have every station in this building check in. Whoever it is they will not get out; I am on my way to you now!" The private quickly responds, "sir, yes sir!" Shortly after that conversation the Captain burst through the doors at the security nest. "Hayes what do you have for me?"

"Sir the download is taking place on 26 West inside storage room 2601, and the guards there are not responding. Whoever it is will be finished in a minute and 30 seconds." Rose wrung his hands in frustration. "Private, quickly scan the grounds for any get away vehicles." The captain grabbed one of the portable radios. "Sergeant Manning what is your team's location."

"Sir we are on 26 east, securing the remaining cargo from the Horizon." The urgency in the captain's voice came through with every word he spoke. "Sergeant we have a breach on 26 west, I need for your team to secure the area and detain anyone you find!" The Sargent quickly responded with a loud "Yes sir!" He turns to his men who were all grabbing their gear. "Okay men you heard the captain, we have some rodents in the nest, time to play exterminator! Dead is detained in my book, so stay frosty! let's move!" The room erupted with a "Oorah!" The men filed out of the room quickly. Suddenly Squirt's voice chimes in on the triplet's earpieces. "Hey, you guys don't have a couple of minutes. You have ten bogies headed your way double-time. Drop what you are doing now; we are headed in to scoop you up!" The scorpion ship was approaching the black site with serious speed, Squirt turns in his chair and shouts with panic. "CB, I can't lock onto the triplet's locations, something is blocking their sensors!" At that moment, Khairi's voice came through the Scorpions intercom, "okay Squirt we are ready, beam us up!" Squirt now franticly working on the screens at his station, blurts out. "Listen guys, they are jamming your sensors we can't locate you to teleport, you need to get outside the building." The triplets looked at one another, Kya with arms out in confusion whispers to her brothers, "outside the building!?" At that exact moment they hear a torch cutting through the disabled locks on the door. Khairi whispers "spread out and take cover we have company." The three quickly disappear behind equipment in the room. Kimoni takes out the power grid on the wall shutting down all lights and electronic equipment in the room. Kya's voice comes over their communications links, "go infrared, and remember they are on our team, non-lethal combat." Khairi blurts out "do they know that!!" Kimoni lets out a sigh, "no, so watch yourselves, and let's all make it home!" their face shields switch to infrared simultaneously. Their earpieces chirped, "come in Ambassadors!!" Khairi responded while watching the men cut their way through the door. "Go ahead CB!"

"Can you guys make it to the roof?"

"Negative CB we have serious opposition closing in on us."

"Okay are there any windows in there, the north side of that room is an outside wall?"

"Khairi responded, confidence briming in his voice, "north wall got it, that's where we will be coming out; and Squirt we will be coming out hot!" Squirt yells, "don't worry Khairi I will be ready." Just then the door flew opened and two canisters bounced along the concrete floor with smoke pouring out of them. Khairi connects three laser prisms together. He whispered in his comm to his brother and sister, "okay crew we are on our way out. Just run for the light!". Kimoni and Kay both reply "cool!"

Squirt shouts "okay guys we are in position and ready let's go!" Khairi whispers "Ok here we come Squirt." The soldiers began to enter the room, with the flashlights on the end of their M 16's glowing in the darkness. Kimoni voice comes in on the group's earpieces, "I count five, definitely a scout team!" Khairi presses the button on the laser prism, a low humming noise starts coming from the prism, and quickly began to get louder. The noise caught the attention of the soldiers. Khairi pops up from behind some equipment and throws the prism at the north wall. A few of the soldier's flashlights follow the flight of the prism. When it hits the wall the flashlights snap back to the area from where it was thrown, but Khairi had disappeared into the darkness. Suddenly the glow from the prism catches the their attention. The lasers activate filling the room with a green light, while completely melting away a huge section of that north wall. As the room began to fill with light and the soldiers were distracted. The triplets jumped into action eliminating the threat from this scout team. Kimoni drops from the top of a file cabinet on the shoulders of one soldier injecting him with a neurotoxin knocking him out instantaneously. He follows the soldier's body to the ground avoiding the light of his partner as he wheels in that direction to see what happened. Kya throws one of the smoke canisters toward the soldiers, then pops up out of the smoke with both handguns drawn unleashing a barrage of neurotoxin darts hitting and dropping three of the men. Khairi takes the brutal approach grabbing the last soldier by his vest. He lifts him above his head and slams him to the floor in one move; he then cracks him across the head with the butt of his knife knocking him out. The triplets take down the five-man team in a matter of seconds. From outside the door, they hear the words BREACH, BREACH!!! Khairi blurts out "A's lets go." The three of them run at top speed for the large hole in the wall created by the prisms. The rest of the assault team enters the room firing at them. They exit the building by jumping out of the hole with no fear as if they were on the ground floor. Khairi was the last one out, he could feel the heat from what the lasers did to the wall as he passed through it. The heat was quickly replaced with the cool rush of air as he began to free fall 26 stories. He quickly noticed that he didn't see the Scorpion or his sister and brother. That was because Squirt was ready at the controls. Khairi could see the black asphalt getting closer fast. All he could do was clinch his teeth; he could only hear the deafening sound of the wind going by. The asphalt now to close for comfort he began to let out a scream. Suddenly a blinding light appears then thud. He was safely on the lower deck of the Scorpion. The sensors for the triplet's lit up like Christmas lights when they exited the building. This allowed Squirt to lock onto each one of them in free fall and teleport them onto the ship. All three of them could hear Squirt yelling from above, "ok CB I have got all three on board punch it!" The Scorpion jets rev up as the ship zips away. "Are you guys ok?" Kimoni still breathing hard, rolls on to his back and shouts, "damn, I thought I was going to die! Squirt you are the man!" Kya chimed in, "yeah Squirt, we are in one piece; I can't wait to see what is so important about this data and metal." Squirt gave a crooked smile while responding, "I am sure Houston will let us in on that." Squirt had made his way from his station to the stairs that lead up to the bridge. He had to see that all three of them were in good health after that ordeal. His pulse slowed and blood pressure returned to normal when he saw the triplets sprawled out on the bay floor one deck below. With sheer relief he made his announcement, "okay guys make yourselves comfortable, we should be back home in a few hours." The triplets each give him a thumbs up signal. Kimoni, was the first to move, he got to his feet and began taking off his equipment; while heading towards the cargo bay. "I need to check on the payload."

Squirt looks back, "it should all be secure Kimoni."

"Not the metal Squirt, the aliens." Squirt froze, "aliens?!" CB shouts from the command center, "did you say aliens Squirt?" Kya interrupts them, "don't ask guys just go with it." She popped up off the floor grabbing Khairi's arm, "come on big bro let's go see if they survived the trip."

Back at the US military black site, Captain Rose and the on-duty staff were waiting to hear back from the containment crew he sent to investigate the breach. Suddenly an agitated voice came through the intercom, "Captain Rose come in." The Captain quickly responded, "go ahead Manning, what do you have?" There was a moment of dead air before Manning responded. He started with a deep sigh, "nothing sir, they got away." Captain Rose responded with a raised voice, "what? What the hell do you mean they got away soldier!?" There was dead air for a few more seconds before Manning replied, "sir there were three suspects in the containment room. They took out a five-man scout crew. Blew a hole in the wall without an explosion. Jumped out of the 26th floor and disappeared into thin air! They also managed to make 2 aliens and a 60-ton case of foreign metal disappear. Sir, we have nothing!" The captain slams the radio on the ground; it shattered into several pieces as he shouted, "damnit!! Hayes get a forensic team up on 26 stat! I want to know about any shred of evidence they find up there!" Hayes tapped his earpiece and ordered a forensic crew as instructed. "Sir the crew is headed up there now, so what do we do for the time being?" The captain chuckled while shaking his head in disbelief, "well, first I need to speak with the Secretary of Defense. I believe Tory's old buddy Houston has poked his nose into our business. It's time we cut his nose off!" The captain stormed out of the room.

The Sonoran Desert, Arizona:

The Scorpion ship disappears into the desert sand as it moves downward on the retractable landing bay. The massive Arizona compound that Houston created was all underground. The compound was complete with living quarters, medical quarters, several labs, offices, storage facilities, training facilities, weapons testing facilities and two retractable landing bays. Inside the compound Kimoni found Houston double timing it to the storage facility that they placed the goods retrieved from the black site. Kimoni took this time to update Houston about the extra cargo they brought back, while Kya and Khairi were keeping them secure. The two of them entered the room, and Houston slowed his pace. He was amazed at what he is seeing in one of his storage facilities. He slowly walked toward the aliens who were sitting in the middle of the room. "Hello, my team tells me you understand English, my name is Houston. What can I call you?" Sigma looked up at him, "hello Houston, I am Sigma, and this is Zeal." Houston was still trying to wrap his head around the fact that he was in a room with extraterrestrial beings. "So, both of you are from the planet called Nova, Nova -lucent?" Sigma could sense most of the people in the room were anticipating something from he and Zeal, he tried to assure Houston and everyone else that they were here in peace. "It is pronounced Novalucent, and yes I am from there, but Zeal is from a neighboring planet in our Galaxy." Houston nodded his head, "so I am just going to ask, is it true that you believe these three," he pointed at the triplets, "have a connection to your planet." Sigma looked at the triplets and gave an eerie looking smile, "yes that is true, from what I have learned from Tory about human DNA; I can tell these three have something from my home world coded into theirs." Houston begins to pace around the room clearly intrigued with what was being said. "That is interesting, and it leads me to another question for you, do your people possess DNA like humans?" Sigma paused to gather his thoughts, "well, it is not that simple, let's just say that we have some similarities in our DNA. The strength of my home world is based on the planet itself. On Novalucent we have an element that can absorb and channel solar energy. This element can be found in the roots of a plant that grows in very remote places. This plant is very deadly to most Novians by touch, smell, or taste, but organisms from the plant can be found in every Novian warrior DNA." Houston gave a puzzled look to the triplets, who offered no response just blank stares. "Okay I am confused, if the plant is deadly, then how the hell do your warriors end up with its organisms in their DNA?" Sigma calmly responded, "our elders share stories of how the planet selects its warriors at birth; because the planet knows which of it's people would make the best defenders. After a countless number of research projects on the subject, we have only been able to isolate the organisms, but we still don't clearly understand how it ends up in select Novian's DNA. We did determine that Novians without the coded organism are no match for those with it." Sigma began to slowly walk across the room toward Houston, "the selected Novians can be identified by the golden circle that forms around their pupils at the age of 3. Once they are identified as a chosen one, they are groomed to be elite warriors for the rest of their life." Sigma was now standing directly in front of Houston. Houston still uncomfortable with being this close to Sigma, slightly stuttered with his question. "Like the golden circles around your pupils?" Sigma nodded, "yes Houston like mine and just like the three you all call the Ambassador's." Houston turns and looks to see the triplets making their way down the hall in deep conversation. Sigma's question brought Houston's attention back to their conversation, "let me ask you, have those three ever traveled to my home world?" Houston quickly shook his head no, "they have never left Earth, and this is our first-time hearing of your home world. The only thing that may come close, we did introduce elements from a comet that may have originated in your galaxy, to their parents. It was our attempt to develop super soldiers but failed miserably." Sigma flashed an awkward smile to that comment, "Houston, I believe the success you were seeking from that program, lies in the bodies of your ambassadors." They both take another glance in the triplets direction, and again, receive three blank stares from the end of the hallway. Houston takes a step closer to the alien, looking deep into his dark eyes; "So, you believe that they have traits of the warriors from your home world?" Sigma nodded yes, "but there is only one way for me to tell; if you would please allow me to run some test with their blood?" Houston paused for a moment considering the request. He reluctantly responds, "I can set you up in one of our labs, what will you need?" For the first time Sigma showed some emotions, his eyes were wide open with excitement, and he could not be still. The stoic persona of the alien melted away. "Some of the contents from my ship were being kept with the metal that was retrieved from the base, is it here?" Houston gave a puzzled look, "yes I believe so." Sigma gave that awkward smile, "good, then I will need some of the ambassador's blood and those contents from my ship." Houston let out a deep sigh, he was praying under his breath that these aliens were here to help and not destroy them. "Okay you two follow me." The compound was equipped with three laboratories; Houston walked the two aliens over to lab 3. He took a glance at Zeal, "you don't talk much do you?" Zeal gave Houston a blank look with a very dry response. "We are very suspicious people; we are open to communicating when we feel a level of trust. Nothing I have experienced on this planet evokes trust." Sigma chimed in, "now that is true!" They stopped at the door for lab 3. This was the smallest lab in the compound and had windows going around every inch of the room. Houston punched in the code to unlock the door. Sigma walked into the lab looking around, "I see this will be where you can keep an eye on us." Houston gave a stern look, "Sigma so far the two of you have proven to be allies, but during these times we must be certain. That trust thing swings both ways, and I cannot take unnecessary risk." Sigma entered the lab, "I completely understand your position. I believe the humans that held us captive were going to make us into a science project, we owe the triplets our lives. As far as we are concerned we are indebted to you all, so let us prepare this room to show our worth to this group." Houston nodded and headed down the hallway. Sigma began checking out the equipment in the lab, "Zeal you will be my link between their world and ours since you know so much about both." Zeal was watching Houston walk away, "that sounds fine Sigma, but do you believe that you can help these 3? Because if we don't I believe these humans will turn on us." Houston reappears now moving double time. He was approaching the lab with a slender black box and three valves of blood. He started talking before he made it through the door, "okay I had their blood drawn; will this be enough?" Zeal responded with a smirk "oh that should be more than enough, right Sigma." Sigma was busy emptying the black case which contained far more contents than the size indicated it could hold. "Yes that will be enough." Houston took a seat as the two aliens began to test the blood; after a few moments Sigma turned to Houston. "Do you have a weapons expert here?" Houston smiled, "yes we do his name is Marcel but we call him Boom." Sigma turned back to the foreign equipment he was working with as he continued talking. "We need him here in this lab; along with the metallic glass you retrieved from the military sight." Zeal, could now finally feel some relief from their experience on Earth; he snapped out a quick statement behind a huge smile, "so we can help them achieve their full potential!" Houston was becoming impatient interrupts Sigma's answer, "so Sigma, what did the test show!?" Sigma stopped what he was doing and turned to face them both, "my tests show that your ambassadors have far more potential than you could ever dream and are far more powerful than you can imagine." He smiled, "Zeal and I will help them reach their maximum potential." Houston stood up, "so they carry a trace of the Novalucent Warrior Gene?"

"Not a trace Houston, they have the gene. We can develop weapons for them that will be very beneficial against the Pernicious. They are the hope for your world against this invasion." Houston ran his hand through his hair, "three versus an invading army does not sound like much hope to me." Sigma began taking new items from the case that came from his ship. He never looked away from what he was doing in response, "yes their armies are usually larger than this, but they were crippled by the battle with my people. That battle cost me my home world and led to one of the Pernicious hives invading Earth. But there is one special thing about this hive, it's the home of their preeminent Queen." He stopped what he was doing to make eye contact with Houston to emphasize this point. "This war will be won by who you kill, not by how many! She is the key to victory and our target." Houston gave a surprised look with his response, "our?"

"Yes our! Believe it or not, Zeal and I are now entrenched with you in this battle!" Sigma went back to what he was doing. Houston was now pacing back and forth in the lab; his growing concern could be heard in his voice. "Okay what you are saying sounds promising Sigma because our military is being overrun by the Pernicious, but I still don't feel confident about any of this. The ambassadors were performing as expected against them until they ran into one of the larger pernicious with tentacles. That was not a good encounter, it hurt Kya bad." Zeal finally felt comfortable enough to join in the conversation, "those large ones are called Guardians. They are their best fighters. Their main job outside of leading invasions is to protect the queen and her offspring. That hive has plenty more of them and they are who we will have to go through to eliminate her." Houston sat back down, "can we, can we really go through those beasts?" Sigma smiled as he saw men wheeling the metallic glass into the lab. "Before now, probably not, but with the upgrades we have in store for those three; they will be unstoppable! Houston I can guarantee that queen will fall to the Ambassador's! Now, we need to get to work." Houston started to exit the lab, "I will get Marcel down here ASAP."

"Great, and Houston I will also need a training center to teach the triplets how to tap into their powers, one that can withstand extreme heat." Houston paused for a second then smiled; "we have the perfect place for that." Houston left the lab to allow them to work, as he walked down the hall he drifted off into a bad memory from six months earlier. A memory that felt all to real. It all started with the onset of the Pernicious invasion. He could still hear the voices like it was happening right now, "Houston come in do you read me?!"

"Loud and clear, go-ahead CB."

"Things are crazy here, our military is taking a beating from these damn aliens."

"What's your location CB?"

"We are circling a private airfield outside of the city. One of the alien ships touched downed there and has not moved for the last hour."

"The triplets are with you aren't they CB?"

"Yes, your newly named Ambassadors will be severely tested here." Houston felt this may be a significant opportunity to learn more about the Pernicious plans for Earth. His best team has a chance to gather some much-needed information about these aliens. The crew he sent was made of Chris Barnes (CB) Captain and pilot, Herman Mills (Squirt) Co Pilot and computer engineer, Marcel Brown (Boom) sniper and explosive expert, Marcus McDonald (Mac) sniper and communications expert, and the triplets Khairi, Kya and Kimoni. Houston's enforcers which are better known as the Ambassadors. Squirt's voice comes over the communications array, "okay we are approaching the airfield and our sensors are indicating a lot of movement around those two large hangers." CB responds, "Squirt cloak the ship and land in those hills East of the airfield. That should give us some cover."

"Will do CB." As the Scorpion circled the airfield the infrared sensors went berserk. "Hey CB, this can't be right I am reading over 10 thousand humans down there."

"Sounds like the sensors are off, they must be reacting to something the aliens have making them malfunction?!"

"Nope, the sensors are working fine. It looks like most of them are located in those hangers, but they are not moving. There are a few hundred of them moving around outside the hangers." Mac chimed in the conversation, "any aliens out there?"

"Yeah, I count about 50 mixed in with the humans but, judging from the size of that ship there must be more than just 50 down there. I just can't tell what the hell they are doing?" Kya gets up from her jump seat and starts collecting her gear, "it's only one way to find out Squirt, did you find us a landing site yet?"

"Yes, preparing to touchdown now, we will be about two clicks from the airfield and totally invisible." CB turns to face the triplets, "okay LISTEN UP! Here is the game plan, we are here to observe and gather information and not to engage the enemy." Khairi stands up, "then why the hell did you bring us? Because if you haven't noticed our military is getting slaughtered out there!"

"Yeah K I noticed, but that still does not tell us anything about what we are facing." Khairi takes a few steps forward, "main damn what we are facing, you heard Squirt, there are humans down there; the way I see it we can knock some alien heads and let the Council pick up the pieces when the dust settles." Kimoni jumps up and slaps Khairi on his back, "I am with that big brother we have not found anyone that can hold up to the three of us." Khairi smiling shaking his head agrees "yeah that is true!" Kya clears her throat to get the attention of everyone, "look Houston put CB in charge of this mission and we are going to let him quarterback it!" Khairi and Kimoni both give her a look of disgust. "Go ahead CB finish telling what you have planned."

"Thanks Kya, like I said we will not engage! Mac you and the triplets will work your way to those hangers and radio back what you find. Boom you find a perch and provide cover if things get squirrely. We need to get as much information as you can about their ship and what they are doing here. Boom, make sure you do your thing and leave some of your gifts on that ship." Boom breaks into a deep sinister laugh. "Those aliens will get to know why they call me boom!" CB clapped his hands like they were breaking a football huddle, "okay guys get in get what we need and get out, do not engage the enemy but neutralize any threats quickly and quietly. Our distress code is yellow got it!" The ambassadors responded with a weak answer of "got it."

"Then move out!" CB shouted. All five of them jumped into action grabbing their gear and made their way down the ramp. Mac positions himself between two boulders and started reconnaissance looking down on the airfield with his monocular. He turns and gives hand signals to Boom, letting him know what direction the aliens were moving. Boom gives thumbs up signal and takes off double time. Mac climbs down, he and the triplets begin moving to get a better vantage point of the hangers. They stop behind some rocky terrain about 30 feet from the fence that surrounded the airfield. Mac, Kya, and Kimoni position themselves where they can see what was happening around the hangers. Khairi squatted down with his back to all of this, completely uninterested in what was happening. Mac broke the silence, "come in CB".

"Go ahead Mac."

"We are about 60 yards from the hangers I spot about 40 aliens; they are actually loading these people onto the ship." CB responded obviously confused, "what!? Mac are the people showing any resistance."

"No but it is clear this is being done involuntarily." Mac moved his leg brushing a few pebbles off a rock, he didn't notice the sound but one of the large aliens with the white hair immediately looks in their direction. Kya under her breath says, "Mac did that thing see us." Mac whispers back "I don't," before he could finish his sentence the large alien turns back to his group and lets out a deafening squeal that freezes every alien. He then points in the ambassador's direction. Suddenly 30 of the smaller aliens begin running at top speed in their direction. Mac shouts "damn, we've been made, so much for a peaceful mission! Scorpion we are code yellow with 30 bogies headed in our direction. Prepare for dust off. Boom what's your twenty?" Just then Khairi stands up; "damn a dust off you all heard our orders. Since they saw us it is time to neutralize these threats." He turns and begins a full sprint toward the 30 aliens headed for them. Kimoni and Kya look at each other in shock. Then they hear Khairi yell "AMBASSADORS LETS ROLL!!" They both look at Mac and give a shoulder shrug, then begin running down the hill behind their big brother. With every step Khairi could feel the ground rumble from the heard headed directly for him. A metal fence was the only thing that separated them, he pops out a couple of laser prisms, with his right hand he activates and throws them at the fence. The lasers cut through the fence taking out a large section and continued slicing through 10 of the aliens.

The bodies of the aliens were sliced into several pieces, and they fell with the sound of raw meat hitting the ground. That sight didn't slow the remaining of the charging aliens, so Khairi kept his charge going. CB's voice came in on everyone's earpiece, "Mac we are headed your way."

"Put your hazard lights on CB, the triplets are neutralizing the bogies."

"Yeah I see that Mac, what the hell happened to a low profile?"

"That big alien spotted us, so the triplets are going to have a chat with him!" CB shouted into the comm link, "Mac we are coming to get you guys I have a bad feeling about this one!"

"10-4 CB, but until you get here I am going to test out this brand-new rifle." CB looks at Squirt and Squirt responds with a shoulder shrug; "okay we will circle the block before picking you up, give them hell Mac!" Khairi leaps over the 10 alien bodies that were sliced and diced by his lasers. He reaches the second group of Pernicious soldiers with his sword drawn, he drops to one knee spins around and slices through the mid-section of one of the aliens. In a continuous motion he sprang to his feet and flipped over the next rushing alien thrusting his sword into the back of its neck. He lands with both of his 40 caliber handguns drawn and began to unload on the rest of the charging aliens mowing them down. Suddenly, he felt someone standing behind him. He quickly spun, falling to his back aiming his guns at this huge alien who was about to smash his skull in with his axe hammer. Before Khairi could pull the trigger, he saw a bullet pierce the alien's throat. Then the air was suddenly painted with the weird color of the alien's blood as four more rounds pierced his body. The alien's limp body dropped to the ground. Khairi sees Kya at the foot of the hill picking off aliens with her side arms. They made eye contact, and she winked at him then holstered her guns and drew her swords ready to join in the fight. She jumped directly toward a charging alien with a sword in each hand, the alien stops and tries to protect himself by blocking her swords with his axe hammer. Too no avail, Kya swung down with her swords, she could feel the vibration as her swords sliced through the alien's hammer and crunched into his neck. She saw the life leave those black eyes as she rode the limp body to the ground removing her swords. The alien's blood flies off the cold steal as she twirled both looking for her next victim. She spots Kimoni in the distance slamming an alien to the ground and silencing him with a dagger between the eyes, but Kimoni didn't realize that he was now surrounded by 5 aliens. Kya shouted, "heads up Ki!!" Kimoni now aware of the situation jumped into action, he rolled over the body of the dead alien to avoid being hit. Then bounced to his feet and in one move pulled two ninja stars the size of his hand from his vest. He smiles at Kya as he activates the blades and threw them forward. The stars glided forward for a few feet then sharply turned one going left and the other right. They flew through the circle of aliens making deep cuts into the necks of one. With each cut you could hear breaking flesh and bones; the bodies dropped around him one at a time. His smile disappears when the last alien blocks both stars with his axe. Kimoni locked eyes with the alien ready to do serious damage. Out of nowhere a blood curling squeal comes from the large white-haired alien. The aliens stopped their attack and began to fall back. The triplets huddle up to regroup. Kya asked, "what do you think they are doing?" Kimoni shouts "I don't know but I bet that big guy with the white hair has the answers we are looking for." Khairi responded, "good then let's rap with him!" Khairi began moving in his direction when Kya reacted with concern, "Khairi wait, let's not rush into this." Kya was correct to be concerned because the Ambassadors didn't know that this large alien was a Guardian. One of the ultimate Pernicious soldiers and, those who encounter them never live to tell. He was approximately 150 yards away and began to take a few steps in their direction, then suddenly leapt and covered 100 yards landing feet from the three. The Ambassadors paused after witnessing that. At that moment all three understood that this would be a battle unlike any other. It was still three versus one and Khairi liked their odds. He shouted, "ok now it is time for you and your alien friends to leave Earth!" The Guardian smiled as he responded, "we will leave this stinking planet once we have collected what we came for, and not before!" Kya asked, "so you are here to collect humans, why?" The Guardian never takes his eyes off Khairi as he responded, "we are here to collect every living organism. You all will be food for our clan!" Khairi shakes his head in disbelief, "that will never happen!" The Guardian responded, "you say that like you have a choice, my Queen has ordained that you either conform or die." Khairi looked back at his brother and sister with clinched teeth and they both nodded in his direction. He shouted at the Guardian, "neither of those options work for us, but the steal of our swords say we have a choice! When I am holding your dead Queens head in my hand you will know what we chose!" The Guardian flashed that eerie smile showing what looked like canine fangs as he moved forward. The moon light glimmered off his axe as he twirled it, he grunted through clinched fangs, "for that human you must go through me and my brethren to get to her." Khairi growing restless with the conversation boldly responded, "that's exactly what we want!" The guardian was still flashing his fangs as he responded, "Then DEATH it will be!!" He quickly struck Khairi in the chest with a thunderous blow with his right fist. The punch sent Khairi flying for about 10 feet. Kimoni and Kya both watched until his body crashed to the ground. They immediately turn their attention to the guardian; Kimoni quickly moved into an attacking position with his sword drawn, he swung it aiming for the guardian's head. The guardian did not move, tentacles came out of the top of both his hands. They emanated from both arms like dark blue rebar, four on each arm. The left tentacle powerfully wrapped his hand and sword stopping his attack. Kimoni was frozen with shock as the tentacle snaped his sword. Then suddenly the right tentacles grab him by his midsection and throws him twenty feet away. Kya could feel her heart racing, both of her brothers had been dispatched quickly by this huge alien. No more underestimating his ability, it was time to empty her arsenal. She twirled both her swords one in each hand, as she plotted out a course of attack. She decided the best course would be to attack while the guardian's attention was still on her brothers. While his back was to her, Kya leaped in the air with her knees tucked under her body. Her arms stretched as far back as possible. Her intent was to plunge both swords into the back of the alien's neck. Without turning around the Guardian reaches back with his right hand; one of his tentacles grabs Kya by her chest abruptly stopping her in mid-flight. The Guardian turned and locked eyes with Kya, as Khairi and Kimoni both struggled to their feet. While holding Kya two feet in the air, the remaining right tentacles wrapped around the rest of her body restricting all movement. The Guardian then turned and smiled at Khairi as one of his left tentacles moved up Kya's body and wrapped around her neck. Khairi sprinted toward the two as the Guardian tightened the grip around Kya's neck. She tried to squirm free to no avail. Her body fell limp as both of her swords dropped from her hands sticking upright into the ground. Khairi screamed "NOOOOOOOOOOOOOOOOOOOOOOOOO!". He pulled out two ninja stars from his vest and threw them as hard as he could. The stars never flew straight when thrown, they would curve and twist with the wind but always find their target. The stars curved out of sight as he continued his sprint toward Kya. The stars reappeared digging deep into the harden flesh of the Guardians back. In shock the Guardian released Kya from his grip and lets out a grunt. He quickly spins to do battle with tentacles exposed. Khairi ducked under the Guardians left tentacle as it swooshes by his head, he took a swing with his sword, but the aliens right tentacle blocked it. The sword broke into pieces on contact. The Guardian bellows out a deep grunt, Khairi could only relate the sound to that of an angry bear. He continued his attack as he pulled his side arm out and let off a burst of 15 shots center mass that push the Guardian back. The bullets bounced off his chest unable to penetrate his flesh, but the alien felt every round. The Guardians right tentacle quickly wrapped around his hand and gun, neutralizing that threat. The two were now at arm's length of another, Khairi pulled a dagger from his vest and quickly stepped forward to plunge it into the alien's neck. He wanted to see this monster suffer for what he did to his sister. His attack was met by three more of the alien's tentacles.

One of the tentacles went through his shoulder one around his neck and the last around his right arm. The more Khairi struggled the tighter the tentacles gripped his body. The alien flashed that unorthodox smile as he dangled him above the ground. He took a quick look at Kimoni to see him staggering back to his feet, then turned to the remaining alien soldiers who were watching the battle unfold. "Is this the best this planet can offer?" The alien troops began to grunt loudly in celebration. He turns Khairi's body to face him, "I told you death is what you shall receive from me, consider this an honor. All hail the Preeminent queen..." Suddenly the blinding lights of the Scorpion ship crested the ridge, and CB unleashed a barrage of bullets on the Guardian and his men. The 30-millimeter rounds were not penetrating the guardian's flesh, but from this range the rounds were very painful. Painful enough for him to release Khairi; which gave Squirt the chance to teleport the triplets on to the ship. Immediately the Scorpion banked hard left and fired its thrusters which blew the Guardian 50 feet back into a fence. "Boom come in; we are headed to get you now! Light your fuse we will need some distractions to keep these aliens off us!"

"I can't light a fuse right now CB."

"What! Why the hell not?"

"Just give me a few more minutes! Are you guys seeing my feed?

"No, Boom we are having technical difficulties with your feed, plus we have a situation on board."

"Damn, you all need to see what's going on down here."

"Down here?, where the hell are you?! Suddenly Squirt interrupted their conversation, "Boom you don't have a few minutes, there are several bogies headed to your position." Boom was inside the hangers, recording what looked like thousands of stasis chambers with human bodies in them. Squirt's statement sent chills down his spine. Boom was so focused on capturing the images in the hanger he lost awareness of his surroundings. He turned to see six aliens with weapons heading his way. Scrambling to his feet to run for cover he screamed in his communications link "Squirt they're no longer approaching I'm taking fire!" He could feel the heat from their projectiles as they whizzed by. The damage inflicted by the weapons assured him that he didn't want any parts of them. Boom saw four very large mechanical cases and quickly took refuge behind them. From that vantage point he could use the windows around the hanger to spot out where the aliens were. He whispered in his com, to conceal his location, "okay CB things have gotten a little too exciting down here. I am lighting my fuse along with a few other diversions. I will be coming out on the east side of the building. Get me the hell out of here!" Boom could see the reflections of the aliens approaching his location. He pulled out one of his specially made cocktails and waited for his opportunity. While the aliens were searching for him around a half-assembled jet that was forty feet away. Boom could see the exit door a few meters from him. He mumbled to himself, "this has to work, this cocktail has to buy me enough time to get out that door." Boom launched the cocktail in the air towards the aliens, and while it was in midflight, fired a round from his handgun. The bullet pierced the cocktail and created a huge fireball. The aliens took cover and Boom bolted towards the exit door. He noticed the door was slightly open, but the hinges were rusty. He let out a yell as he threw his left shoulder into the door, "Aagghhh!!" The impact was vicious, the door flew open with some of the rusty hinges breaking off. Boom's momentum took him to the ground where he rolled over and stopped his body on one knee. "damn that door was heavier than I thought," he said trying to rub the pain away from his left shoulder. His shoulder pain was quickly forgotten about because the noise from the door drew the attention of the aliens outside. A group of them began to approach Boom with their weapons drawn. Boom suddenly froze as a blue light surrounded his body. The aliens paused for a few seconds, confused by the light, then unleashed a barrage of shots as Boom disappeared and the wall received all their fire power; leaving gaping smoldering holes in it. Suddenly the Scorpion screamed by overhead, and the aliens turned their fire onto it. CB shouted, "did we get him!?"

"Yes, CB everyone is on board now just get us the hell out of here." Boom was laying on his back on the deck floor, he quickly began patting his body checking for wounds. He found none and exhaled for what felt like the first time in hours. He dragged himself off the floor and made his way up the stairs to the bridge door of the Scorpion. "I saw Kya and Khairi back there they both look to be in rough shape."

CB responded without looking back, "you may want to strap in because we need to get them to medical support ASAP!" Squirt turned to Boom, "so what did you see in that hanger that had all your attention?" Boom takes a deep breath before answering, "there were some types of chambers down there, thousands of them." Squirt blurts out, "by chambers, you mean chambers with more aliens in them right?" Boom shook his head no, "no Squirt they were putting humans in them, like they are collecting us for something." Astonished by those words CB turns away from the ship's controls, "wait say that again Boom?" Boom took another deep breath, "yeah, believe it or not the hanger has an underground storage that was littered with thousands of chambers for as far as I could see. Main, what the hell are we facing with these damn aliens?" Boom mumbled while taking a seat in one of the empty navigational chairs. CB ran his hand threw his hair, clearly frustrated. "We just can't get ahead of them, to many unknowns, they're too advanced for us. We have to get ahead of them to defeat them!" Boom let out a deep sigh, "yeah I get that CB, but we learn something about the aliens every time we battle them, eventually we will find their weakness." CB bounced up out of his Captains chair. "Squirt let me know when we are close, Boom let's talk." The two walked out of the bridge into the hallway. Boom started talking before the bridge door closed, "come on CB calm down we will get a handle on things." CB looks around to make sure no one can hear him. "I am not so confident in that Boom. These aliens have giant warriors that took down the triplets with no problem. They are shredding our military. Their weapons are more powerful than anything we have ever seen. Our shields barely withstood their ground forces fire, what happens when their ships start firing at us?" Boom hesitated before responding. He looked up to his right like he was vividly picturing a memory, "yeah I saw their fire power up close it was horrifyingly impressive." That statement excited CB because he was now 3 inches from Booms face with hands on both his shoulders. "So, you feel me, we all know what happens in history when two civilization's meet and one is far more advanced." Boom quickly takes a step back, "whoa, I am not ready to write the human race off just yet. The triplets were handling those aliens until this huge one showed up right." CB frowned at that statement, "that's true but they could do nothing with the big one. Hell, I even fired on him from the Scorpion and the 30-millimeter rounds did nothing. Those rounds would slice through anything else but with him they just drove him back, no serious damage at all!" Boom rubs the top of his bald head while letting out another long sigh. He paused for a moment contemplating what he just heard. "CB we have more powerful weapons." "Yeah Boom but what if those weapons don't stop them?" Boom shrugs his shoulders, "then we get the triplets to capture some of their weapons; I guarantee their own weapons will be affective against them! CB, I know these are unprecedented times, but one thing will never change, we don't lose!" He said with a raised voice. "Now let's get back on task we need to get the injured to Paulina so she can get them back on their feet." CB took a long look down the stairs of the ship where Mac and Kimoni where nursing the injured. "I get that Boom, but this just feels different." Boom stops halfway down the stairs and looks back, "that is because it is different, we just can't panic!" CB took a deep breath, "I hope you are right, because if we lose God only knows what plans those beasts have for

Earth. One thing is clear, humans aren't included in those plans." He turns and walks back to the bridge. Boom takes a seat on the stairs with his face in his hands.

He could feel the despair in every fiber of his body, the realization that they were all in real trouble just punched him in the gut. The triplets were the best they had to offer and if they were unsuccessful in battling these aliens, what chance do the rest of them have going forward. He heard CB open a communication line, so he eased back up to the doorway of the bridge to listen in. "Base come in." The unmistakable voice of Houston came through the receiver, "base here CB, what is your status?"

"Houston we are headed your way; sir we need Paullina to prep the med lab. Kya and Khairi were injured during the fight with one of the aliens." There was an uncomfortable pause in the conversation before Houston responded, "did you say they were both injured, how bad?"

"Bad enough for them not to be able to heal during the battle. We are a few clicks out, and we have a briefing about the aliens for you when we arrive." Again, there was an uncomfortable silence before Houston responded. "We will be ready when you get here." The Scorpion touched down on a helipad in the middle of the desert. Once the ship engines stopped the helipad began to descend below the sand. Two huge brown concrete slabs closed above the descending ship concealing any evidence of a helipad. The ship stopped some 30 stories down; the hatch of the Scorpion opens to reveal a five-foot three-inch, brown skin curvy silhouette with jet black hair. She was dressed in blue camo print scrubs and a long white coat. It was Dr. Lopez; Squirt was the first to see her. He froze in the doorway. Her large beautiful brown eyes were peering at him over the top of her black rimmed glasses. Her Spanish accent was like music to his ears when she spoke. Herman was so enthralled in the sight and fragrance of Paulina he didn't focus on what she was saying until she yelled his name. "SQUIRT!!" He inhaled deeply before responding, "oh hey Doc, what's up?" She responded like a teacher speaking to a fifth grader, "where are my patients?" Squirt steps away from the hatch opening, pointing toward the stairs he blurted out, "they are below in med bay S1." She grabbed him by his arm to pull him out of the doorway, so her staff could get to the wounded. Five people with two anti-gravity stretchers zip by. Inside the ship Paulina asked, CB and Kimoni, "what the hell happened out there?" She continued to stare at Khairi for an answer. Kimoni's voice sounded defeated when he answered, Paulina had to strain just to hear him. "We were doing reconnaissance and our position was compromised, the aliens started their attack, so we all went to work. We were not having any problems until one large alien with white hair showed up. Our weapons were ineffective against him." Khairi who was laying in the chamber next to his sister, strained to sit up due to the injuries he suffered.

The whole time Paulina was asking her questions, Kimoni never took his eyes off Kya while holding her hand. He mumbled under his breath, "Mac managed to get her hooked into this medical chamber and she has been stable ever since. Khairi let out a loud grunt as he got to his feet, to look up and see all eyes fixed on him. His response startled the room, "I saw something different in that thing eyes. I saw complete death and destruction for us, if we don't eliminate these aliens now, then life as we know it will soon end!" The room fell silent, everyone had now come to the reality that these aliens will not be easily dispatched. Paulina breaks the silence, "how are her vitals?" Mac quickly responded, "they are weak, but slowly improving." Paullina begins to check her breathing and pulse; "her breathing seems labored." She shouts orders to her staff, "let's get these two to the med lab stat." Squirt grabs Paulina by the arm, "hey doc, those two will be okay right?" Paulina gave a concerned look, "I won't know exactly what's going on until I get some x-rays. So let us get to work, I will let you all know something soon." Paulina and her staff briskly moved off the ship with Kya and Khairi on stretchers. CB stepped back into the bay door and sternly announced, "Houston is waiting for the rest of us for debriefing." The crew made their way to one of the nearest conference rooms, where they found Houston. He was sitting in a chair facing the door. CB led the group into the room and Houston greeted them, "come in and have a seat and Boom close the door behind you." CB, Mac, and Boom took seats on the first row, while Kimoni sat in the back of the room. Houston started the conversation, "so, correct me if I am wrong, we have two Ambassadors in the med lab from the hands of one alien on a reconnaissance mission. Do we need to revisit the definition of reconnaissance?" The room remained silent; the only sound was a low hum from the HVAC system. Houston stood up from his chair, "at least there were no casualties on this mission. What if anything can you tell us about these aliens since you all had an up close and personal view?" Kimoni spoke up from the back, "most of those aliens were no problem, but that large one gave us all pure hell." Houston paused to let that last statement sink in. He then slowly moved to stand next to the front row, starting a 3d video from Booms suit camera. The 3d images were displayed from projectors on the ceiling and took up the entire front of the room. Everyone sat in silence as they watched the shaky video, feeling like they were reliving Boom's encounter. Houston spoke over the low-quality audio, "we do have a little research on these aliens; they have been named the Pernicious because of the path of destruction that follows them everywhere they go. After today I am sure it has become painfully obvious, that we are truly in a fight for the survival of the human race!" Houston paused the video on a shot of the chambers that were on the lower level of the hanger.

He turned to face the group before making his statement. "The chambers that you see here from Boom's recording are for humans. They have been setting up places like this all over this planet. We are the reason they are interested in Earth. Believe it or not we are a food source to them." A loud, "what!" Erupted from the group. Houston continued, "they survive off the life source of other beings as they travel from galaxy to galaxy. Those chambers are simply storage compartments for humans." CB shouted, "how many different worlds have encountered these Pernicious?" Houston let out a deep sigh, "based on the little information gathered by our military they have dominated thousands of worlds. Each planet that they invade becomes a farm for their home world and they slowly bleed the planet for all its inhabitant's life until there is nothing left. Then they move to their next targeted planet." The room fell silent. Everyone was attempting to process what they just herd. Houston ended the video and turned on the lights. "Right now, our only option is to somehow get ahead of their technology and weapons." Mac threw his hands up in disgust, "how do we get ahead of them?"

"That's a great question Mac, and I believe the answer to that is in a black site in Virginia. Word is the Horizon brought back some special items that may prove to be very beneficial to the ambassadors." Kimoni leaned forward in his seat, "Houston with all due respect, at this time shouldn't our focus be on stopping these aliens, hell we need to be working with the military?" Houston shot a stern look in his direction, "Kimoni right now it is in our best interest to limit our exposure to the military because of you and your siblings. They will always consider you three as their property, and I will not have that. As for the material, it is some form of metal, and it possesses an opportunity to create more powerful weapons. Those weapons in your hands can be enough to stop these aliens, which is why it means far more to us than them." Houston's wristwatch buzzed, he tapped it, and it projected an image of what looked like hospital documents. He looked through them quickly then swiped them away. "Okay we will handle that mission really soon for now let's go check on your sister and brother." The crew all rose from their seats and began to make their way to the med lab led by Kimoni. He entered the med lab and was pleased to see Kya sitting up in her bed. He quickly moved across the room to her side, "K how do you feel?" Kya clearing her throat before responding, "hey big bro, I am very soar, and I can't really remember what happened, but other than that I am fine. Please tell me at least 100 of those aliens did this to me."

Kimoni shook his head no, as he answered, "it was that damn big guy that did this to you."

Kimoni took a hold to Kya's right hand with both of his, "this will never happen to the three of us again; the next time we cross paths with any of those aliens we will leave them in pieces!" Paullina enters the med bay and interrupts their conversation, "excuse me Kimoni, but your sister needs her rest." Kimoni turns to Paullina, "so doc, how long before she is 100 again?" Paulina stopped jotting down Kya's vitals to answer, "well she had severe trauma to her spine, neck, and rib cage; but we were able to stabilize her, and her body took over from there healing itself. It looks like she will make a full recovery. I still want to run a few more test before I release her." Khairi who was now moving around with less pain entered from the back of the room, "thanks doc, I don't know what we would do without you." Paulina flashed a slight smile, "well gentlemen I did not do much, it really is the amazing ability you three have to heal your own wounds."

It was Mac screaming his name down the hall, "Houston! Houston!!" that snapped him out of his daydream. He took a second to get his bearings before responding, "yeah Mac what's up?"

"You must see what Sigma and Zeal have done, we have new weapons, all around! Weapons that are just as powerful as the Pernicious. We need your help to upgrade the guns on the Scorpion." Houston paused for a split second. Maybe this was the glimmer of hope they were seeking. This could be their chance to get ahead of their alien technology and change the trajectory of this fight. He shouted back, "I'm on my way, but where are the triplets? Mac gave him a huge smile from ear to ear, "they are with Sigma in the Climatic Chamber testing their new weapons, and the chamber can barely hold them." He franticly signaled to Houston to hurry up, "come on main, you have to see this." The two quickly made their way to the secluded part of the base where the chamber was located. They turned the corner to see Boom standing outside of the chamber bay window, holding up a case of orange bullets. The explosions inside the chamber shook the entire building. Boom shouted at Houston, pointing at the bullets, "we all have some new tricks for those damn aliens!". Houston peeked in the chamber to see the triplets training with a newfound confidence. He turned back to Mac and Boom, "that is great to hear we have an edge, let's get finished because the faster we upgrade our weapons the sooner we introduce those aliens to death!" Mac and Boom responded with a loud resounding "HELL YEAH!!" While the two weapons experts made their way to the weapons depot, Houston signaled for Sigma to come out of the chamber. Sigma exited the chamber with what looked like a smirk on his face; Houston realized that he had not seen an expression like that since they have met. "I see your new-fashioned weapons are working with the triplets." Sigma looked back through the glass at the training, "they have exceeded my expectations, it's like they are true Novalucent warriors. They just need to learn how to manage their capabilities! That will come over time." Houston folded his arms across his chest, "I do have a few things that I am concerned about. You said it is not how many, but who we kill, do you really believe that killing their queen will stop the invasion?" Sigma turned to face Houston, "I had some time to ponder that, and I believe the best course of action is to kidnap the queen and negotiate a cease to the invasion." Houston paused, thinking about that option, "why kidnaping and not killing?" Sigma smirk quickly turned back to his stone face look, "this group is the Alpha colony, and they travel with the queen and her daughter. Killing the queen would not stop their attack and killing them both would be impossible. By kidnaping the queen, we put their colony in jeopardy.

The life of their nest, which you consider to be their ship, is contained in her. Without her the nest loses the ability to sustain the members of their hive, resulting in catastrophic deaths. When the princess takes reign of the throne, the makeup of the nest changes to protect her. It will reject 90 percent of the hive and rebuild with the strongest 10 percent." Houston holds up a hand to stop Sigma from talking to respond, "right now all I hear is the queen's death increases our chance to win this fight!" Sigma shook his head in frustration, "the smaller their colony the less life sources they need, which means they will unleash their wrath on us. The rejected members of the hive will seek to destroy this planet, for them that would be an honorable death. The results, I believe your people call it scorched Earth. But it will be a million times worse than you can envision. My people were able to destroy some of their colonies and that cost us our home. Is that what you want here?" Houston was frozen from information overload, there was far too much weighing on this one decision. He needed more time to figure out a solid plan, time that he didn't have. The Pernicious were ripping through every major city on this planet with very little resistance. Time was running out, and this was their best shot. While staring at the ceiling Houston took in a deep breath and slowly released it. "So, Sigma if we do this kidnapping thing how do we keep the queen secure?"

"Well Zeal and I created a containment field with the metallic glass from my home world. She will never be able to penetrate it, nor will their sensors detect her inside of it." Houston turned and started walking toward his office as Sigma followed, "okay what about transport, we will need to move her?"

"Yes we also constructed shackles and a mobile cell with the same properties as the containment cell here on site; they both will work in the same manner." Houston stops walking to look back at Sigma. "Do you believe this will work?" Sigma paused for a moment, choosing his words carefully before answering, "the Pernicious are not the consensus type of species. They are more of a everyone complies to their way." Houston chuckled, "was that even an answer?" Sigma looked around to make sure they were alone. "Houston; I have no idea of what will happen, but this is the best shot for you to get them out of this solar system peacefully. Just be prepared for anything, because one thing is certain, they do not take losing well." Houston ran his hands through his beard, "how long before we go?" Sigma handed Houston a tablet, "you can see here, CB was able to gather intel that their main group is headed for the white House. One of their rituals is brutally killing and displaying the bodies of the most powerful leaders of those that oppose them." Houston gave a look of confusion, "you can't mean President Taylor, he and the joint Chiefs are safely tucked away!" Sigma took a step closer to Houston and scrolled down on the tablet, "the intel CB received confirmed the reason they are headed to the White House is for a meeting with President Taylor." Sigma stepped back and firmly stated, "we will need to intrude on that meeting!" Houston dropped his head in disbelief, "Jesus, I have got to get the team ready!" Houston was flustered from that information, with both hands on his head he mumbled, "how much time do we have?" Sigma tried to calm him, "CB and Squirt have been working out the logistics and time frame since they found this out. We have a day to get everyone briefed then make it to Washington, and they." He said pointing at the triplets who were still working out. "Are ready, they are just waiting for orders! Don't over think this just let them unleash their talents." Houston offered no response, he quickly turned and sprinted down the hall leaving Sigma behind.

12:15 PM Washington D.C.

The doors of the oval office were ripped away and the Guardians violently entered. The aliens were moving so fast that they just appeared as grey streaks of light. President Taylor was brushed back to the front of his desk by something moving past him. The streaks of light and crashing sound of furniture was overwhelming for Taylor. Suddenly there was eerie silence, as he looked around the room the guardians had every human except him bound with their tentacles. None of his soldiers managed to get off a single shot during the melee.

Taylor was clearly shocked at how these aliens overpowered his protection so quickly. Fighting back panic in every fiber of his body, he stood up straight, straighten his clothes. He began to step forward in anticipation of another alien with tentacles coming through the door for him. Instead of that he watched as their Queen entered the room. Taylor clinched his teeth to quail the sense of desperation that was reaching out for him. He found himself staring at her blue skin, she seemed to glide into the room. Her bright red eyes were piercing, he felt a strong urge to look away but couldn't because that would be interpreted as weakness. President Taylor cleared his throat to begin a dialogue. "We are here under an agreement to just have a discussion with you." Queen Azieal threw her hand up to silence him, "no, you are here because we have the location of your so-called important leaders. This is an effort to prevent the inevitable!" He was amazed at how well she spoke, but that was part of the Pernicious process for invasion. They immersed their clan in the culture of the unfortunate subjects that were their targets. It was a sick way of displaying their dominance without it being any misunderstanding. Taylor calmly offered a rebuttal to her statement, "so, are you saying that we cannot have a discussion here about peace?"

"Peace?" The Queen chuckled as she uttered the word. "They call you the President right?" Taylor was confused by that question; he had no doubt that she knew who he was. He answered sternly, "yes I am the President of the United States, and this is." The queen raised her right hand again to cut him off. "Do you know anything about us?" President Taylor paused before answering, trying to figure out where these questions were going. "Well yes, we know that you are called the Pernicious by all that encounter you." The queen began to walk around the oval office as she spoke, it seemed as if she was measuring the space to move in. "So, does that name Pernicious mean anything too you?" Taylor still confused gave a dry response, "yes it is the name you were given by your enemies based on the wicked and destructive acts you perform!" The queen gave a look of disbelief to that answer, "you call us wicked, let me ask you Mr. President, is it wicked to ensure that your people have the necessary essentials to survive? Is it destructive to destroy your adversaries to secure your species survival? How can you consider that wicked when human history is littered with such acts? The evil you say we spread is for the purpose of our survival; while you humans commit evil against one another because of beliefs, land, and wealth. Which of those acts sound wicked to you?" Taylor realized that this was not a conversation but a declaration, and he wanted to calm things down. He responded with a humble tone, "well, before we go any further with this conversation how shall I formerly address you?" The queen stopped her prance around the room, looking the President directly in the eye and responded with a stern, "I am Queen Dylan the supreme leader of the Pernicious." President Taylor gave an unimpressed look in responding, "well Queen Dylan we can debate the merits of evil for hours or we can address the real issue, which is the fact that your armies have invaded our territory. We came here on today in hope of an opportunity of peace, a possible opportunity for our people to learn from one another." The queen moved to be directly in front of the President. She looks around the room before responding, "your response to us should be on bended knee, either now or in a pool of your people's blood. We have already sent you into hiding and I have not unleashed the full might of my military yet. So, let me ask you what in our history makes you believe we came here in peace? We have adopted the name Pernicious because it describes our superiority to all things in all universes. You have no defense for us, this world was mine before you were born and will be until your bones become dust! Surrender now and eliminate the blood shed for your people, or we will continue to obliterate your military." Dylan turns to one guardian and nods, and he brought a chair and set it in front of the desk for the President. With the palm of her hand Dylan slowly pushed the President in the chest forcing him to sit in the chair against his will.

Outside of the White House an anxious Mac reaches out to their headquarters. Houston's commlink chirped to life with Mac's voice, "Houston it's getting really hairy in there we need to move." Houston could feel the anticipation as he leaned in closer to the 3D digital display, it was clear that time was running out for President Taylor. He knew the Ambassadors were their only hope. He shouted into his comm, "no stand down, the Scorpion is two minutes out; you two just let CB lead the resistance! Is that clear Mac!?" Mac responded with a weak, "yes sir."

Back inside the oval office, the Pernicious Queen leans down to get right into the President's face, "now, Mr. President it is time for you to announce the surrender of your people and lead the rest of this rock to follow you." Taylor now looking up into her red eyes, blurts out loudly in response. "No, never!". Dylan leans in closer; he could only see emptiness in her eyes; her skin gave off a strong musk order like a wild animal. This close he could clearly see the dark blue fangs as she smiled at him before speaking. "No! Good, then I will place your body on a stake on the front lawn of this building! We take what we need for our survival and now your planet and its people are what we need!" The President smiles, "you will soon learn that we are a people who are not easily defeated." The alien queen begins to pace around the room again with her response. "Perhaps you have been blinded by the puny humans who cower in the shadows of this so-called powerful place, but for decades we have conquered thousands of worlds far more advanced than this little blue rock. We have never tasted defeat!" President Taylor struggled to his feet, turning to face her, "you have never tasted defeat because you have never faced humans before! That ends today!" Dylan lets out an awkward laugh, "so Mr. President I take that you are sticking with your answer to our request for surrender." President Taylor slowly walked around his desk, looking at all his men still being held in bondage by these aliens. He could not help but feel despair as he was trying his best to fight it off. He leaned forward placing both hands on the desk and mustered the strength to say, "the United States never has and never will negotiate with terrorists, and we do not know the meaning of surrender!" The Queen smiles, "that's unfortunate Mr. President, because it's obvious that you don't pay attention to your own history of first encounters? The more advanced civilization always exterminates the weaker, now I am sure it is not difficult for you to guess which one of us is the weaker." She let's out that eerie laugh again, as the other aliens joined in. Taylor thought to himself their laughter sounds like a pack of hyenas. The queen suddenly stopped laughing and continued her point, "you really thought this was an opportunity for mediation between us. No, this is us planting our flag on the building that represents power to your people. What do you call yourself the leader of the free world, the so called most powerful man on this rock called earth? You will simply be made an example of how powerless your world is against us. Mr. President it's now time for you to signal the end of the human race!" Taylor stood up and straightened his clothes while walking around his desk toward the queen, "do what you will to me but understand that from this day forward you and your people are in a fight for your lives!" Osen intercepts the President restraining him before he could reach the Queen. Taylor thought, if I only had a weapon I could end her right here. Taylor could feel his blood begin to boil, he shouted, "I may never see it but you and your goons will fall to human hands!! You will never erase us; your children will bury you, and their children will bury them before this is over!!!" The queen looked around the room, "erase you," the queen responded. "Silly man, humans will always be here to serve my people. What else do think they will feed on?" She paused letting that statement sink in. She then leans in close to the President's right ear, "okay it's time for us to get started. You will be executed on the front lawn for all to see." She stands up straight and shouts, "let us show this planet that all their hope just ended on today!" She looks at her lead guardian, "Oseen bring just him and signal the nest for full invasion!" Oseen snaped to attention with a growl, "yes my Queen!" Queen Dylan turns on a dime and exits the oval office followed by her chief guardian Oseen restraining and dragging the president. Those three exited the room leaving the rest of the Pernicious guardians with the remaining security team for the President. As soon as they reached the hallway President Taylor could clearly hear signs of struggling and human voices screaming. His heart dropped right then because he knew he was alone and about to see death in a horrifying way.

Outside of the White House, Houston hears Boom's voice break the silence no longer trying to whisper. "Come in Houston!"

"Yeah go-ahead Boom"

"You see what is happening, either we move now or there will be no reason too!" Houston let out a long loud sigh, "yeah Boom the...." Just then CB interrupted their conversation. "Mac, Boom we are coming in hot. Mac I need for you to get in sniper position to give the Ambassadors some cover!" Mac quickly responded, "I'm already in position CB! Houston you know we weren't going to wait right?!" You could hear Houston fighting back a smile as he spoke, "yeah I figured that." CB broke into their conversation with more instructions, "Boom I need you to disable that ship and keep it on the ground." You could hear over the comm link that the big guy was on the move in his response, "got you, just look for my fire works!"

CB spins around in his flight chair to face the back of the bridge. "Ambassadors I am sure you want to show these pernicious your new shiny weapons." Kya stood up, "more than you will ever know CB, we owe those guardians some payback!" CB spoke through clinched teeth, "good that's what I wanted to hear; now capturing their queen, dead or alive is our main objective but getting the President to safety is a huge bonus!" CB spun back around in his chair to face the ships controls and started a broadcast to everyone on their channel. "We're a few blocks away from our targeted location! Our approach will be from the east with the ship cloaked. Hopefully they will not be expecting any hostiles!" His voice began to rise from anticipation, "okay folks, here we go, this will be hard and fast so be ready! We will drop the Ambassadors on the White House front lawn. Squirt you man the guns and help Mac push back any alien soldiers leaving that ship on the ground. Our new MGX weapons will be a welcome surprise for them!" The left side hatch to the Scorpion slid open; you could see the tops of the trees zip by as the ship headed straight toward the pernicious ship. The triplets stood there anxious to get on the ground and capture their queen while rescuing the President and cracking a few alien sculls on the way. Suddenly they hear Squirt blurt out. "Oh no!" CB shouts, "Squirt what's wrong?" Squirt responded with panic in his voice, "their ship has locked on to us." Everyone on the ship gave a puzzled look, as CB stated the obvious. "Even with us cloaked?"

"YEAH EVEN WITH US CLOAKED!" CB took a deep breath, "Okay, we knew this wouldn't be easy." He turned to the Ambassadors, "guys they know we are coming so there will be no element of surprise. They will be ready for you." The triplets smiled simultaneously, and Kya responded. "CB they may be expecting us, but they will never be ready for us!" Kya then turns to her two brothers and ask. "You two ready to hunt!?" The short loud response she received from both was simply "Born!!!" Kya then turned to the open hatch, "then let's roll." Their eyes began to glow as each one of them exited the ship, first Khairi who exited by falling headfirst out of the ship into a ball. Kimoni was second, he took a couple of steps and fell out of the hatch backwards into a back flip. Then finally Kya, she turned and leaped out of the ship in a swan dive. Mac and Boom were fascinated at how much ground the three covered in free flight. The triplets were wearing newly fabricated WX2 combat suits. The suits were now made from the Novian metal, they were lighter, flexible and 50 times stronger than Kevlar. The suits were also upgraded with the latest and greatest technology. The triplets could feel the wind zipping by as their helmets heads-up display gave them a glide path and landing zone. The suits were also equipped with small thruster jets that slowed their descent to the ground. They each landed about 150 yards from the entrance of the White House. Standing between the pillars of the north doorway was Dylan, Oseen and President Taylor. The princes Sadu and several more guardians were making their way up the stairs to the queens left. There were several foot soldiers exiting the ship that destroyed all the vegetation to the right of the White House. The Queen smiles at President Taylor while pointing in the direction of the Ambassadors, "these three again; Oseen it seems as if they are very persistent." Oseen gave a head nod, "yes my queen it does seem that way." With an irritated tone she orders, "do away with them now!"

"My pleasure my queen!!" Oseen quickly responded. He then motions to three of the guardians and the alien soldiers to attack. They all turned and bolted in the direction of the triplets with the three guardians leading the way. Kya was the first to react, her eyes and swords began to glow bright orange, as she surprisingly began sprinting toward the oncoming aliens. She headed directly for the guardian warrior leading their pack. As they reached one another she leaped in the air, but this time she was prepared for his tentacles. The guardian stopped and released all six of his tentacles straight up at Kya's feet intending to snatch her out of the air. She used the tentacles as a springboard to flip over the guardian, while holding both her swords like butcher knives in her hands she impelled them through his body from the back. Purple blood flew out of the alien's chest, he used his tentacles to stable himself as he looks down to access the damage. Kya wanted to send a message to all the Pernicious seeing this; she wanted this alien to fall hard. Still holding on to both of her swords with her feet now on the ground; she sprung up using the alien as leverage and flipped her body up with her feet landing on his shoulders. While staring into his red eyes she pulled out both of her A.R. carbine pistols. She then pushes off jumping backwards, the force of her jump made the alien stumble back a few steps which put him in the perfect position for what she had planned. A loud continuous crackle filled the air as she unleashed 6 rounds from each of her guns. The recoil from each shot seemed to keep her in the air as if she was levitating, defying all the physical laws of gravity. She fell to the ground, watching the MGX bullets rip through the tough alien skin, with the last going through his head. His lifeless body fell to the ground. While that was happening, Kimoni singled out another one of the guardians. As he ran toward him with his gun in his right hand he let off two rounds piercing the left shoulder of the guardian. The pain stunned the alien stopping his approach to Kimoni. Seeing an opportunity Kimoni let loose with his gun emptying the clip. The guardian extended all six of his tentacles creating a protective barrier like a web from Kimoni's bullets. The 30 rounds stung the alien, but mostly doing minimal damage. Once the barrage of bullets stopped, the alien retracted his tentacles to see Kimoni a foot away airborne with is left arm drawn back. That was the last image the guardian would ever see. Kimoni expected the guardian to use his tentacles as cover, so he never stopped his charge using the gun fire to keep the guardian stationary. While charging he reached up behind his head with his left hand and grabbed the handle of his sword, with the alien blinded he angled his attack to the left. He drew his sword and once he was in striking distance the alien revealed his upper body. Kimoni leaped in the air and with one sweeping motion he detached the aliens head from his body. Now Khairi had his own choice of showing what he and his siblings were capable of. While his brother and sister tangled with their opponents, the guardian facing him drew an axe. Khairi immediately hit the thrusters on his suit which shot him across the lawn directly for the guardian. It happened so quick the alien was not able to protect itself and Khairi hit him square in his midsection like a linebacker. He separated the guardian from his axe and in one motion ascended straight up. The guardian began fighting back by hitting Khairi in the back and using his tentacles to destroy Khairi suit. Khairi quickly countered the attack by doing 3 quick 360 turns to disorient the alien; after reaching 50 feet he then flipped and threw the alien toward the ground. The guardian flipped head over heal a few times before it used its tentacles to balance and land safely. The problem was Khairi was closely following the alien's descent, holding his sword over his head with both hands just waiting for the alien to land. The guardian's tentacles took the brunt of the fall, but as soon as his feet touched the ground Khairi was impaling him through his neck. His sword went through the lifeless body as it fell to the ground. The rest of the pernicious froze with astonishment from what they just witnessed from these so-called puny humans. The ambassadors took a moment to smile at each other enjoying their work before they turned up the heat, opening fire on the queen and princes as they sprinted forward. The Pernicious amazement was interrupted by the whizzing bullets from the ambassadors and Mac's guns. This time the fight between alien and human was taking on a different look and feel. The humans were now on the attack; Oseen shouted to his men "retreat and protect your queen!" The triplets were now running at top speed toward the building, unleashing a barrage of bullets that were piercing the alien's tough skin like it was wet tissue paper. Queen Dylan was frozen with shock, realizing that her display of domination was not going to happen as she thought. She looked out over the lawn to see three of her guardian's lifeless bodies littering the ground; she knew something drastic had to happen fast. "Oseen what the hell is Happening!?" Oseen was now moving the queen toward their ship, "my queen it seems as if their weapons have been upgraded we need to move you to safety now!" Oseen shouted orders to their foot soldiers and remaining guardians, "secure the princes and get her to a safe place!" Someone in their ship was paying attention to what was happening and began firing some nasty bullets at the triplets forcing them to seek cover and slowing their pursuit. The cover fire gave Dylan, Sadu and their men the opportunity to retreat to their ship. The confusion gave a second team of Navy Seals the opportunity to rescue President Taylor and slip back into the White House; rushing him to the panic room. President Taylor could hear the remaining aliens in the building hastily making their way to the front entrance to join the fighting. The men managed to keep the President out of sight. Suddenly the ambassador's earpieces came to life with Boom's voice. "The President's clear; we are a full go for capture! Hey Mac, did you run out of bullets? I haven't seen you drop any aliens lately!" Mac screamed back, "If you haven't noticed I am busy not getting shot by one of those huge guns on that ship! Where the hell are you?" Again, Boom's voice inflection indicated that he was on the move, "me, oh I am just preparing the entertainment!" You could clearly hear his smile in that statement. Kya responded, "entertainment what entertainment Boom?!!" There were a few seconds of silence before Boom responded no longer on the move. "Just get your guns ready, you will have a lot of bad guys to drop right about now!!!!!" A loud earth-shaking explosion happened at one of the ships landing stanchions. The explosion forced the ship to slowly tilt to its right side before they fired thrusters to balance it. The shrapnel from the explosion forced the Pernicious to take cover. The momentum just shifted and the ambassadors along with scorpion ship began their barrage again. This time the three were firing directly at the queen and her men, while the Scorpion kept the alien ship busy attempting to slice it in half. The guardians were surrounding the Queen and her daughter protecting them from the bullets with their bodies. The bullets were shredding their bodies but not making it through the protective barrier of alien flesh to the ladies. Suddenly Khairi launched an RPG directly at the group surrounding Dylan. One of the wounded guardians realized what was coming and pushed the group towards their ship while snatching the RPG out of the air with his tentacles. While moving in the opposite direction from the group; he pulled the RPG into his body, covering it with all six of his tentacles to protect his people from the blast. The explosion blew him back into the group escorting the princes to the ship. His body knocked a soldier and the princes back towards the White House doors, separating them from her protection. Dylan stops her group and calls out to her daughter, frantically signaling for her to come with her right hand, "Sadu hurry, and get back to our group!" Sadu could not make out what she was saying, her body was still covered by the lifeless guardian that saved her life. She struggled to get free from under the 290-pound body on top of her, as she watched her mother's group be teleported onto the alien ship. She realized then that her sensor was damaged from the impact with the guardian, that's why she was not included with the group. She noticed that things were quiet and assumed the gun fire had ceased, she mumbled out loud, "my people will come back for me shortly." It turns out the gun fire had only paused; the Scorpion was making another run unleashing a barrage of bullets on the alien craft. The bullets were ripping through the hull of the ship doing considerable damage. Still freeing her body from the lifeless guardian, she spoke to who she thought was one of her protectors, "wait, how are their weapons now able to penetrate our shields? What is happening?" Sadu was complete befuddled. What she didn't know was, Mac's explosion not only severely damaged the ship, but it also disabled their shields. To avoid further damage the pernicious ship had to launch without Sadu. It had to pull some quick maneuvers to avoid the onslaught of fire they were taking from the Scorpion. Sadu could feel panic set in after seeing her people leave her, she manages to free herself from the lifeless body, exerting all her strength. She took a moment to gather herself in the mist of her fallen protectors, when she notices some feet stop where she was. Not recognizing the gear as pernicious, she slowly looks up to see the three ambassadors standing over her with all six of their AR Carbine guns aimed. Kimoni smiled and said, "I bet you were not expecting this on today." Kya blurts out on the comm link, "we didn't get the Queen, but we do have the princes, we need a ride before her ships circle back." Khairi kneels and violently slaps the restraints on Sadu with a huge smile. "Welcome to Earth!" CB voice interrupts their fun, "turn around, we are already here." They quickly get her on her feet and drag her onto the ship. Squirt yells to CB, "we are clear to go, let's move because company is coming fast." Everyone scrambled to secure the princes and buckle in. CB punched the thrusters on the Scorpion to make an escape, but there were two Pernicious sidewinder ships on their tail. Both ships were firing on the Scorpion attempting to disable it. CB shouted, "Squirt put everything we have into our rear shields; I will have to lose them!" Squirt tapped a few buttons on his control panel and shouted back. "You better do something quick because our shields won't last much longer, and those ships are capable of pinpoint maneuvers at high rates of speed!" CB smiled as he looked over to Squirt, "yeah but they can't fly like me!" He pulled the stick on the ship back toward him sending the Scorpion ship into a climb; gravity slammed everyone's body into the back of their crash seats. They were now headed directly for the belly of the Pernicious ship they forced to liftoff. Alarms began to sound on the Scorpion, "proximity alert collision ahead." CB fires the thrusters increasing the ships rate of speed toward the hive hull. Everyone grit their teeth fighting to breathe with the gees they were pulling. "Quick question" Kimoni grunted through his teeth to CB with his voice shaking from the vibrations of his chair, "did this just become a suicide mission? Because you do know that we won't do any damage to that ship; they'll just scrape our remains off the hull!" CB quickly responds, "calm down people and enjoy the ride, hey Squirt are the bandits pulling back?" Squirt shoots a puzzled look with open hands to the ambassador's before answering, "no they're actually gaining ground!" CB smiles, "good." Squirt now staring at the back of CB's head, "what the hell do you mean good, we're stuck between a rock and a bolder there's nothing good about this." CB continues to snatch the ship from left to right not giving the alien pursuers a clean shot at their thrusters. "Everything is not as it seems young one." Just then the ship's computer blurts out an alert, "target lock, evasive maneuvers immediately!" Squirt hits a few keys on his terminal and the alert shows on his screen. He shouts, "we've been targeted by the big ship with no forward shields, prepare for serious impact!" Before anyone could react to what Squirt said, CB immediately snatches the stick banking the ship left, slamming everyone into the right side of their chairs.

Squirt forced his words out through clinched teeth, "CB we are going too fast to bank like this! This path puts us directly in the firing path of that big ass cannon!" On cue one of the cannons from the lower side of the ship fires, a large blue ball with a trail of light was headed for the Scorpion. The on-board computer chimed in, "prepare for impact in 6, 5," The triplets scream "CB!!!!!!" CB suddenly flipped a switch initiating maximum reverse thrust, everyone's crash seat harnesses tightened keeping them from being thrown forward. All but CB's limbs floated up towards the top of the ship. Their bodies felt weightless for a moment. The tail of the Scorpion dipped down; it looked like the ship was frozen in time as the two Pernicious ships blew past them making drastic maneuvers to avoid a collision. The maneuvers forced one of the Pernicious ships to lose control spinning out. The second ship flew directly into the firing path of the cannon taking the full brunt of the blast from their own mothership, just like CB planned. CB abruptly levels the Scorpion, while turning in the opposite direction and punched it. The thrusters snatched everyone into the back of their seats as they made their escape. Squirt cloaked the ship while CB contacted Houston.

"Houston we are intact and headed your way with package in tow!" Houston let out a deep breath in relief as he responds, "ten four CB!"

On the Alpha 13 nest. The Preeminent Queen was in her quarters pacing back and forth. She could not believe the position that they find themselves in. She witnessed the capture of her daughter and a part of her Guardians division severely defeated. There were very few examples in history of the Pernicious being in this position. This was the first for queen Dylan. The only planet that has ever made this type of stance against their assault was Novalucent. She could not understand how these puny humans were fighting with the abilities of Novalucent warriors. She could hear her remaining guardians down the hallway preparing for their meeting. Her clan now faces an unknown future. She doesn't know who survived the blast on Novalucent and if they are friend or foe. The only nest that she knew escaped was Azieal's, but there were millions of stars that separated the two of them. Dylan stood there frozen staring at her reflection in the window. She had come to the realization that the survival of her people would be an exceedingly difficult and precarious road ahead. Her train of thought was interrupted by one of her Guardians. "My queen we are ready for you." Dylan turned and just stared at him not saying a word. Her facial expression showed her anger at being disturbed. She spoke in a very stern tone, "I WILL BE IN WHEN I AM REDY! Is that understood!!!!" The guardian nodded his head as he quickly backed out of the doorway, "yes, my queen." He shut the door in a hurry. Dylan had to regain her composer before she entered this meeting with her remaining leaders, to have a conversation about surrender. A word that was taboo with her people. She slowly began to make her way from her chambers to the throne room. The hallway walls that led to the throne room had golden statues of the previous twelve preeminent Queens lining both sides. She could only wonder what her place in the history of the Pernicious will be after these events. As she entered the room her nine Guardians stood, and she made her way to her throne. She took a seat and made the announcement "let us start." The highest-ranking guardian Noi began speaking. "My queen we have been in steady communication with those humans that are holding Sadu in bondage. They have not changed their demands; they want us out of this galaxy." Dylan shifted in her chair out of frustration in hearing this, "do we know how they are able to keep her imprisoned? By now she should have burned their facility down!" Noi hesitated before responding, understanding how tense this conversation was. One wrong step and he would find himself face to face with the barrel of a weapon. "This is an assumption, like their weapons these humans are using Novian technology, that is how they are holding her and why we cannot locate her." The queen again shifted in her chair, looking very uncomfortable. "Then what do you suggest Noi?" Noi looked around the room before responding, "my queen, I suggest we regroup and lay waste to that entire place, after we retrieve Sadu!" Dylan tried not to show any doubt with her statement, "what I just witnessed was nowhere near our way, these 3 humans are an irritant to me." Noi responded in tone of disgust, "I am certain surrender is not an option my queen?" Avo the guardian who disturbed her in her quarters interrupted. "My Queen if I may say something?" Dylan shot him a puzzled look for speaking out of turn. He replied to that look with stammered speech, "I may have a bit of good news." She let out a deep-toned growl, "right now I can use some good news, what do you have for me?" Avo stood up while bowing his head in the direction of Dylan. He looked around the room before speaking, "my queen, we have been able to contact Azieal's hive." The queen shifted all her body weight forward to the edge of her seat hearing that. She asked with excitement in her voice,"What is their status?"

Avo now feeling comfortable after the reaction of his queen to his news, began to speak with confidence. "They are 10 million light years away with damage to their hyper drive, but their nest is healthy and anxious to fight for the preeminent throne. We have the equipment needed to repair their hyper drive!" Dylan rose to her feet and smiled at Avo. "Thank you for that information." She opened a channel so that the hive could see and hear the rest of their discussion. Every pernicious around the hive froze, listening intently. She firmly states, "Noi, contact the humans and ask what we need to do to get Sadu back, and make sure we meet all their demands." The entire room gasped. Dylan had to respond, "I need all of you to understand that this is not a surrender just a little retreat. Those so-called Ambassadors surprised us with their new weapons. That won't happen again, once we secure my daughter, we will go to the aid of Azieal. After that," she stopped to stare at the image of Earth rotating above the middle of their table, then pointed at it with her scepter. "We will return to this rock, and those three ambassadors along with every person on this planet will feel the overwhelming presence of the Pernicious!" She let out a brief howl, then shouts, "THEY WILL FEEL OUR UNRELINTING RATH!! WE WILL LAY WASTE TO THIS PLACE! NOTHING WILL SURVIVE!!" Hearing those words, the guardians leapt to their feet and began responding by banging on the table and walls while letting out a deafening group howl. This response felt right to her, it was a sense of normalcy in the midst of turbulence. She raised her scepter above her head and the sounds from her guardians in the room grew louder. Suddenly the walls began to shake around the room as the howl began to spread throughout the hive. Dylan could feel the vibrations flow through every inch of her body. She smiled as she thought, "this feels like the Pernicious that I know!" She snarls and flashes her fangs to her guardians, because she knew this moment would lead to the end of Earth.

EPILOGUE

President Taylor, Vice President Mason, and Secretary of Defense Jaffer all entered the observation room in a hurry. Everyone in the room jumped to attention. President Taylor took a moment to look around the room and take everything in. The room was built with stadium seating, the first three rows of seating had been converted into three long workstations with computer terminals looking down on a wall sized video screen. President Taylor saluted the men and women and said, "at ease." That statement snapped them all back to what they were doing. Colonel Drew Suggs who was seated below the workstations, began to make his way up the stairs. Before reaching the top of the stairs Suggs began greeting the men with an update of their status. "President Taylor, Vice President Mason, and Jaffer, thank you for joining us, we have everything set up for you down here." The men began to walk down the stairs as Suggs continued his updates, "Mr. President, our drones are in place, and we will be able to see and hear everything that happens with the exchange from here." The three men followed the colonel to their seating area. President Taylor expressed his disappointment in the operation. "Colonel, I don't like watching vigilantes handling operations that should be run by our military." Suggs is a 5-foot, 5-inch tall, brown skinned balled headed man with a deep booming voice. He was known by his men as a reserved leader, but the President's statement caught him off guard. A little frustration began to show as he responded. "Sir, neither do we, but since the group called the ambassadors were the ones to capture the alien princes during your rescue. The Pernicious specifically asked for them and no one else." Taylor let out a deep grunt, indicating his displeasure. "Again, our military should be present during this exchange," he said sternly while looking at Jaffer. The colonel, sensing the elevated tension in the room tried to deflect. "Well Mr. President, the Pernicious set the terms and location for this exchange. They specifically asked that only the Ambassadors be present and nothing but unarmed drones within 30 miles to document the event. Anything else will cancel the deal and we will be back to square one, invasion." The President shook his head no, still not accepting the reasoning. He spoke with an elevated tone so the entire room could hear. "Jaffer after all of this is over, I want a sit down with Houston and those Ambassadors!" Jaffer quickly responded, "Sir, that is already in the works, once we finish with this exchange!" That statement was received by silence and a direct stare from the President. The silence and eye contact were very uncomfortable for Jaffer, he turned to Vice President Mason hoping for some support. Mason took the hint and walked closer to the scoreboard screen they were sitting in front of; he cleared his throat to break the silence, "so colonel what more information can you give us about this exchange?" The question startled colonel Suggs; he was preoccupied with studding the obvious discontent the President had for this operation. "Uhm, well sir, like I said the Pernicious chose the location of the South Pole. We believe they think the limited amount of sunlight would reduce the ambassador's special abilities and strength." Mason turns back to face the colonel with a look of concern, "are there any apprehensions about the ambassadors doing this with limitations?" Everyone's attention shifted to the colonel for a response. Suggs, tried to choose his words carefully, in an attempt to not add fuel to a smoldering fire. "Well, to be honest, we have several concerns about this operation. I expressed those concerns and Houston vehemently said the ambassadors would be ready for any and everything." President Taylor offered a "hum, so you spoke with Houston?" The President shot a fiery glance at Jaffer before turning back to Suggs. Colonel Suggs could now feel the Presidents eyes burning a hole through him. At this moment he completely understood the gravity of this operation. After suffering the devastation of a full-scale invasion and watching friends and family members gathered like herds of cattle to never be seen again. The people of earth needed to see a symbol of human victory, to see some hope for the future. It needed to see these destructive aliens, tucking their tails, and leaving earth. This operation that Suggs orchestrated, but no longer had control over could be Earths only chance. Colonel Suggs began feeling sick when he realized what was left of his career was in the hands of the ambassadors. His thoughts were interrupted by the voice of a staff member, "sir we are detecting the Scorpion ship on site." Colonel Suggs turned and looked the man up and down a few times before responding. "Thank you private, put everything on this screen," he said while pointing at the front wall. "We don't want to miss anything!" President Taylor added. "Sir yes sir!" Was the quick response from the private. The Colonel, President, VP and Secretary of Defense all took seats in front of the screen to see the ambassadors exiting the scorpion ship with their prisoner. The ambassadors were all dressed in white hooded trench coats that they wore over their normal gear. Under their hoods they wore white turbans and scarfs covering every inch of their face and necks. The smoke grey heads-up display goggles that they wore to protect their eyes, stood out in contrast to all the white clothing and snow. This was the only thing that could be used to identify the triplets in the video being displayed. The pernicious princes was still in her restraints with an oversized orange cover to protect her from the cold air. Kya was the first to notice a ship heading directly for them, she shouted to her brothers, "heads up here they come!" The ship was one that had not been seen in the alien fleet. It was much smaller than the fighter ships that at one time was covering the sky. To Kya the ship reminded her of a stingray fish made from rough dark blue granite stone. The ship slowly approached and circled the entire area looking for any threats before touching down. Queen Dylan and a guardian exited the ship walking towards the group, Kya grabbed Sadu by her right arms as she led her and her brothers toward the aliens. They stopped four feet from one another. Dylan never took her eyes off her daughter, she asked, "Sadu are you ok?" Kay removed the orange hood and quickly responded for her, "She is fine, now take her and go!" Dylan stood in silence with an icy stare towards Kya. Kimoni stepped forward, "what is with the delay, gather your package and leave now," he turned to Kya and said, "remove her restraints Kya." Kya turned Sadu to face her and released her restraints. Sadu quickly snatched the orange cover off and threw it down at the feet of Kimoni. She then snarled at the three and blurted out, "this is not over!" Turned and walked to embrace her mother. Khairi picked the orange covering up and tossed it in the direction of the mother and daughter while responding, "it better be over because if any of your species come back to Earth, there will be no more captures, it will be to the death!" Dylan and Sadu, look back at the triplets without breaking their embrace, and for the first time the ambassadors see them both smile. Flashing their sharp blue fangs. Kya now staring directly at Dylan, "smile all you want, but if you breathe Earths air again, I am putting your head on a stake." Dylan gave a simple head nod and turned as they walked back to their ship. The triplets took a moment to relish this accomplishment as they watched the alien craft rise into the grey sky until it was no longer visible. Khairi opened his commlink, "CB we are read, his voice trailed off as he pointed to the left of Kya and Kimoni. A jet-black void the size of a doorway appeared from nothing. Kimoni was the first to react as he drew his guns, "those damn aliens double-crossed us!" Khairi shouts "hold on K, let's make sure, these are aliens!" Just then four bodies step through the void dressed in grey and white winter camouflage with matching helmets and face shields. Kya turns back to her brothers, "this can't be?" Just then a weird voice came from the group, "ambassadors lay down your weapons and surrender now!" Kya lets out a chuckle, "it's the freaking government, what do we do?!"

Khairi stepped forward with a quick answer, "we will not surrender for sure! K, holster your guns we will do this hand to hand if they don't take no for an answer. There is no need to let the world see us laying down our own military." He jumped back on his comm link, "CB we need you now!" CB responded with a frustrated tone, "give us a sec, we have some F-sixteens targeting us!" Turning off his com link Khairi mumbled "damn, this won't be quick. Okay guys follow my lead." Khairi gave their answer to the agents, "we do not surrender and never will, just go back into your little black hole and this won't get physical!" The largest of the four agents was clearly the one speaking, with a voice that sounded like a recording. He was obviously the leader of the group, and his response surprised them. "Then it will be option two!" Three of the government agents began moving over the snow toward the ambassadors. Kya smiled and winked at her brothers and said with excitement, "ok, option two, let's go!" The ambassadors were making quick work of the three agents until the big guy joined in. Khairi was having trouble with him; it was as if he anticipated every move Khairi made and countered it.

The big agent managed to land a crushing blow to the right side of Khairi's head with his stun baton. The impact cracked his goggles, and a pool of blood could be seen forming on his scarf. Khairi now dazed and frustrated, pulled down his hood and snatched off his head gear, exposing his bloody face to the cold air. The big government agent froze when he saw that. The pause in his attack was long enough for Kimoni to land a head shot cracking his visor. The agent removed his helmet. The triplets couldn't do anything but stare at what they were seeing. The agent, with a look of utter confusion on his face, dropped his baton and began to fumble with a bracelet on his right arm. Suddenly another black void identical to the one earlier opened behind him. He took one last look at the triplets, and he simply stepped into the void, and it disappeared. He left the other three agents behind, whose unconscious bodies were sprawled out in the snow. Kimoni tapped his ear to open his comm link again, he spoke with a confused tone, "Houston did you see that, what the hell was that!?" Kya chimed in, "Houston the real question is who the hell.." Houston and Nicole were watching the exchange on tablets in their Arizona compound. Houston interrupts Kya's question with a stern voice, "ambassadors delay all communications now this is an open channel with unwanted ears! CB is in route; we are now in shadow protocol!" He abruptly disabled all communications and feeds, then turned to Nicole with his mouth gaping wide open. She looks at him then back to the tablet to see the triplets swiftly moving toward a half-cloaked scorpion ship while destroying their comm links. Nicole let out a soft chuckle and mumbles, "there is no way in hell I'm believing in what I just saw." Houston, shaking his head in disbelief, slams his hands onto the tablets crumbling them and shouts, "our Government is unfreaking believable!"

CONTINUED IN
EARTH'S GUARDIANS -
VOLUME II